T0357533

Summer

Can you ta…

Love is in the air and the forecasts have promised a spell of sun, sea and sizzling romance. So let us whisk you away to this season's most glamorous destinations full of rolling hills, blissful beaches and piping hot passion! Take your seat and follow as seven sun-kissed couples find their forever on faraway shores. After all, it's been said you should catch flights, not feelings—but who says you can't do both?

Set sail on the canals of Venice in…

The Venice Reunion Arrangement
by Michelle Douglas
Available now!

And look out for the next stop of your travels with…

The Billionaire She Loves to Hate
by Scarlett Clarke

A Reunion in Tuscany
by Sophie Pembroke

Their Mauritius Wedding Ruse
by Nina Milne

Dating Game with Her Enemy
by Justine Lewis

Coming soon!

THE VENICE REUNION ARRANGEMENT

MICHELLE DOUGLAS

Harlequin

ROMANCE

Harlequin®
ROMANCE

ISBN-13: 978-1-335-21640-3

The Venice Reunion Arrangement

Harlequin Enterprises ULC
22 Adelaide St. West, 41st Floor
Toronto, Ontario M5H 4E3, Canada
www.Harlequin.com

Printed in U.S.A.

Recycling programs for this product may not exist in your area.

Michelle Douglas has been writing for Harlequin since 2007 and believes she has the best job in the world. She lives in a leafy suburb of Newcastle on Australia's east coast with her own romantic hero, a house full of dust and books, and an eclectic collection of '60s and '70s vinyl. She loves to hear from readers and can be contacted via her website, michelle-douglas.com.

Visit the Author Profile page
at Harlequin.com for more titles.

To my dear friend Kerri Lane, who welcomed me into my local romance writing community back in the mid-1990s. A huge thank-you for all of your support, for the laughter, but most of all for your friendship. Love you to the moon and back.

Praise for
Michelle Douglas

"Michelle Douglas writes the most beautiful stories, with heroes and heroines who are real and so easy to get to know and love.... This is a moving and wonderful story that left me feeling fabulous.... I do highly recommend this one, Ms. Douglas has never disappointed me with her stories."
—*Goodreads* on
Redemption of the Maverick Millionaire

CHAPTER ONE

'THE NEXT ITEM is a real treat. We're delighted
to have partnered with renowned portrait artist
Hallie Alexander to auction a two-hour portrait
sketch. Hallie needs no introduction, and we're
thrilled to have her as part of this year's charity gala.'

From her seat at one of the VIP tables, Hallie
managed a polite smile. Despite the hyperbole,
she suspected the majority of people in the ballroom weren't familiar with her name. Though,
as the emcee read out a list of her credentials,
even she had to admit they were impressive.

She'd painted portraits of some of Australia's
most well-known faces, from the ranks of old-
money high society through to an eclectic bevy
of celebrities. Five years ago, her entry in one
of Australia's most prestigious art prizes had
won the People's Choice award and now hung
in the National Gallery. Three years ago, she'd
taken out the top honour in the same award.

That portrait was now housed in an esteemed private collection.

Several sections of the room sat a little straighter in their chairs, recognising the prestige beneath the hyperbole—that a portrait painted by Hallie Alexander had cache, was a status symbol. And as she'd discovered in the past few years, status symbols mattered to some people. A fact that tonight's charity auction took full advantage of.

'Good,' she murmured, careful to keep the smile on her face. Suicide prevention was a cause close to her heart.

Her mother's death from an overdose of sleeping pills when Hallie was sixteen had been pronounced accidental, but Hallie had always doubted the ruling. Her mother had surrendered to despair and had sought oblivion. End of story. Which was why Hallie was here this evening. If she could help raise a few pennies for such a worthwhile cause, then she would.

Actually, she hoped to raise more than just *a few pennies*.

When she'd first started out, a two-hour portrait sketch would've cost the sitter two hundred dollars. She crossed her fingers. Tonight she hoped to reach five figures. She didn't do sketches any more, and maybe that would be a point in its favour, have it considered a rarity. She crossed the fingers of her other hand.

These days she focused on portraits in oils. It

was what she truly loved and where she'd started to make serious money. *Go me.* Some days she had to pinch herself. This kind of success was everything she'd ever said she wanted.

Not everything.

She released a long, slow breath. No, not everything. She'd once sworn to take the European art world by storm. Instead, she'd run away from London with her tail between her legs, had returned home to the safety of Sydney.

The bidding started at a flattering two thousand dollars. Five figures reached just like that. She sat up a little straighter, gave herself a little shake. Was she really ready to call game over on her European dream?

If she wanted to achieve it, now was the time to push herself out of her comfort zone. Either that or shelve the dream for ever. Deep inside, the girl she'd once been scratched and clawed at the walls Hallie had built around her.

For the first time in a long time, she forced herself to consider the notion seriously. Why shouldn't she resurrect that dream? She'd left London because of Lucas Quinn, but that was seven years ago. She'd given up enough of her dreams to that man. Was she really going to give up this one, too?

The thing was when she'd been dreaming this particular dream, she'd always thought Lucas would be at her side.

A familiar ache took up residence in her chest. It didn't matter how often she told herself he could never have made her happy. She'd never been able to shake the man from her head or her heart. One person shouldn't have such a huge impact on your life. It shouldn't be allowed. *She* shouldn't have allowed it. Her mother had provided her with the perfect example for exactly how foolhardy that could be.

The bidding rose to ten thousand dollars.

Ten thousand?

Was it a sign?

Go out there and achieve big things. Stop holding yourself back.

'The bidding is at fifteen thousand dollars to the lady at table fourteen.'

Holy crap!

They did realise it was *only* for a two-hour portrait sketch, right? Admittedly in whatever medium they preferred, but still… She glanced at the big screen and released a slow breath. That *is* what it said up there in big, bold letters.

A bull-necked man raised the bidding by five hundred dollars. She did her best not to scrunch up her face. She knew his type. He'd try to bulldoze her into a full portrait. She didn't let anyone bully her, but it'd take a ridiculous amount of tact—not to mention time—to extricate herself from his demands.

She bit back a sigh when the room remained silent, reminded herself it was for a good cause.

Someone else must've raised a paddle, though, as the bidding rose by another five hundred dollars.

Mr Bull-Neck immediately thrust his paddle in the air, wielding it like a battle-axe. Yep, a bully.

You let Lucas bully you.

She had not!

Though she *had* believed his lies.

They'd been engaged for God's sake! Why wouldn't she believe him? And anyway, she suspected he'd believed them, too. It was why they'd been so damn convincing. But that made her a fool, not a wimp. As soon as she'd realised how empty Lucas's promises were, she'd walked away.

Run, more like.

For heaven's sake, give it a break.

All of this had happened seven years ago. Time to let it go. The fantasy she'd woven around him had dissolved like fairy floss in the rain. Why taunt herself with old dreams?

Pressing her hands together, she reminded herself that Lucas would've made her as miserable as her father had made her mother. *That* was what she needed to remember. *That* was what she needed to focus on. He might've made her feel as if she'd been at the centre of his universe, but that had been a lie.

Focus on the reality.

And her current reality was a star-studded charity event, and she ought to be paying attention.

Mr Bull-Neck's paddle swung a little too close to the polished up-do of one of his neighbours. The woman's glare, though, went unheeded as he brandished the paddle again.

A tall man at the back of the room stood. There was something vaguely familiar about him. The light was behind him, though, so she couldn't make out his features. But the broad line of his shoulders... She frowned. The way he held his head...

'One hundred thousand dollars!'

He didn't shout but his voice rang around the entire ballroom. The sound of the air leaving two hundred sets of lungs followed immediately afterwards. It wasn't the sum, though, that had Hallie gripping her hands so hard she was in danger of cutting off the circulation. It was the voice.

The voice belonged to the man who still haunted her dreams.

Lucas Quinn.

Oh, God. Don't do anything stupid. Like run over there and throw your arms around him.

Or race from the room. Or throw up. Behave like an adult.

Forcing her sagging body back into straight lines, she did what she could to respond to her table companions' congratulations, pressed a hand to her heart and smiled, pronounced herself flabbergasted. But beneath it all, her heart hammered and her pulse twitched and flinched like a skittish cat. The refrain *Lucas is here, Lucas is here, Lucas is here*, went round and round in her mind.

What was he doing in Sydney? Bidding on a sketch? From her? For a hundred thousand dollars!

Recalling the look on his face the last time she'd seen him, she had to suppress a shiver. He'd said he'd hoped to never clap eyes on her again. And he'd meant it.

He wasn't here to make peace; of that she was certain. He'd *never* forgive her for walking away from him. When she'd walked away, he'd have excised her from his heart and mind with the same brutal efficiency he was known for in business circles. A hard ball lodged in her stomach. He'd always had more important things on his mind than her.

So what was he doing at a charity ball? Bidding on a two-hour portrait sketch *from her*?

The question plagued her, but as the emcee introduced the next item up for auction—a pretty diamond bracelet—and the bidding began, she couldn't very well leave her table to go and ask him. What were the protocols once the auction was over? Should she approach him and thank him for his support, or should she wait for him to approach her?

Good Lord, what was she thinking? Neither of those things would eventuate. Lucas would leave when the official part of the evening was over and the dancing began. He'd leave her hanging like he always had. It had been his MO seven years ago, and she couldn't see that having changed in the intervening years.

That realisation made her pulse slow even as her heart gave a sick kick of recognition. Her questions wouldn't be answered this evening. Lucas would make an appointment for the sitting when he was ready. She'd find out what this was all about then. Not a moment sooner.

So when the official part of the evening drew to a close, she refused to so much as glance towards Lucas's table; refused to watch her expectations be fulfilled as he stalked from the room. Not that she had much opportunity to glance anywhere. She was swamped with well-wishers congratulating her on receiving such a high sum for her sketch. The charity organisers, utterly delighted, attempted to get her to sign on the dotted line for next year's auction while euphoria ran hot in her veins—if only they knew the truth!—and the gossips wanted to see if they could squirrel some tasty titbit from her.

Did she know that Lucas Quinn was ridiculously wealthy, that he'd built a financial empire through innovations in nanotechnology, that he lived in a palazzo in Venice, that he was insanely good-looking?

Yes, she did, thank you. Not that she said as much, just smiled and nodded and made the appropriate noises at the appropriate intervals. She blew out a long breath when the crowd around her finally thinned, and she surreptitiously glanced at her watch.

'I'm afraid it's a little early to be racing off home and curling up with a good book. Especially when you're one of the stars of the evening.'

The voice came from directly behind her and all the fine hairs at her nape lifted. Her breasts prickled with a sudden surge of awareness.

Behave like an adult.

Pasting on a smile, she turned. 'Hello, Lucas.' She wondered if she should add, 'It's nice to see you.' He'd see through that, though. But for form's sake... The man *had* just forked over a hundred thousand dollars to charity.

For a portrait sketch. For two hours of her time. It made no sense.

'You're surprised to see me. Shocked even.' His voice held a hint of an Italian accent that hadn't been there when they'd been engaged. In the same way, she supposed, her Australian accent had lost the hint of English brogue it had once had. 'To the core,' she agreed, and had to suppress a shiver at the savage satisfaction that briefly lit those dark eyes.

He didn't say *Good*, but it was written there for her to see, and she read the subtext. Because he wanted her to. He wasn't here to reignite their old romance.

Did he really think her guilty of harbouring such hopes?

'It would be polite of me to ask you to dance, but…'

She raised an eyebrow.

He shrugged. 'You never could dance.'

Some sixth sense told her he wasn't trying to be offensive, but it was clear he was finding politeness difficult to achieve. For some reason, that gave her heart. 'And clearly, dancing with me is the last thing you want to do.'

'The very last,' he agreed and then frowned, chagrin chasing through his eyes, and it almost made her laugh.

Lucas had always held himself to impossibly high standards. He might want her to know that he took no joy in seeing her. He might want her to know he had no interest in her whatsoever. But he wouldn't want to lose his cool. He wouldn't want to look anything but calm and collected.

And she would *act like an adult* if it killed her. 'Thank you for your very generous support of tonight's charity. The organisers are thrilled.'

Firm lips pursed. 'Suicide prevention was always a cause close to your heart.'

She'd confided to him her doubts surrounding her mother's death. Her mother had been smart in so many ways, but not when it had come to her love life. Hallie had no intention of making the same mistake.

Lucas didn't move away. Something throbbed behind the darkness of his eyes. He had something he wanted to say, and she wanted a drink. 'If you don't want to dance then perhaps you'd like a drink?' She gestured towards the bar.

He swept an arm out in front of him. 'Lead the way.'

It took every ounce of poise she had to keep her movements smooth. But she was aware of the way the silk of her dress slid against her skin as she walked, an enticing warmth spreading from the centre of her belly and radiating outwards.

They reached the bar and she had to lock her knees to stop them from shaking when the smoky spice of his aftershave wrapped around her. She ordered a glass of champagne. He requested a whisky sour. In the old days they'd have ordered pints of bitter.

He stared into his glass with lowered brows. She burned to know why he was here, but refused to ask. Instead, she lifted her glass in his direction. 'I believe congratulations are in order.'

An eyebrow rose. 'Because I won your portrait sitting?'

'No, Lucas,' she said gently. 'It's been seven years since I saw you, but in that time you've achieved everything you set out to—beyond even your wildest imaginings. I know how hard you've worked. Congratulations on your success.'

She couldn't read his expression. Very slowly, he lifted his glass and touched it to hers. 'Do your insides now burn with regrets?'

Said insides scrunched up tight. 'For?'

'Knowing that if you'd had the patience and fortitude all of it could have been yours, too?'

Fortitude? For a moment she gaped at him. She'd had a miscarriage for God's sake! Had he really expected to snap his fingers and make all her grief just disappear? A grief he'd never shared, though he'd been careful to hide that fact.

In that moment, she found some of the closure she needed to put this man behind her for ever. She knew exactly what she was going to do. She was going to start a list. She'd record all the reasons why walking away had been a good idea seven years ago. She'd keep it somewhere handy where she'd see it every day. And the first item on that list was going to be *Lucas considered my miscarriage a blessing in disguise*. Second item would be his bitterness.

It was seven years ago. Let it go, bro!

And it was time to take her own advice.

Face it, woman. When it came to Lucas, you dodged a bullet.

She started to laugh with the relief of it. 'Oh, but of course, Lucas,' she said with a mocking tilt of her head. 'Every single day. When I wake in the morning it's my first thought, and my last thought when I turn in again at night. I've not had a moment's peace.'

Shaking her head and still chuckling quietly, she waved her fingers at him and turned to leave.

'Wait!'

What the hell was he doing needling this woman when what he wanted was her help?

'Please?' Lucas managed through gritted teeth.

She halted, but didn't turn around.

'I apologise. I'm acting like a petulant child.'

But seeing her again hurtled him back seven years. Back to when he'd had total faith in her.

He'd had girlfriends prior to meeting Hallie, but from the moment he'd met her it was as if a key had clicked into place, as if the planets had aligned, as if fate had brought them together. He'd thought she'd stick with him through everything. He'd thought that together they'd overcome anything.

Never in a million years would he have believed that she'd break his heart. He'd been a fool.

Seeing her now, tonight, all of these years later—looking even more beautiful than she had back then, pulsing with an inner vibrancy and still as out of reach as she'd ever been—made him realise his heart had never fully healed. There were fault lines in danger of fracturing again. A sobering fact as this woman had never been worth the pain he'd suffered.

And yet, he'd suffered it all the same. To realise he was still vulnerable, still in danger of repeating the same mistakes, was a slap to the face. Especially when he'd thought he'd eliminated her from his system—thoroughly and ruthlessly.

He fought the urge to turn around and walk away. It galled him to the core that he needed her help. But he'd do anything for Enrico. Even this.

'Seeing you again has taken me unexpectedly off guard. I apologise for my rudeness.'

Her shoulders rose and fell as if on a breath. Or a sigh. She turned around. 'Not all the memories from seven years ago are bad, Lucas.'

He resented her. He resented her poise. He

hated that she could still make him feel so vulnerable, but he reminded himself that she'd never been mean or spiteful. Hallie just hadn't had the grit or fortitude—the patience—to go the distance.

She leaned a hip against the bar and lifted her glass to her lips, took a sip, her eyes never leaving his. 'Do you want to tell me why you're here and why you bid on my prize?'

It was an invitation, an opening, an easing of the way. As he'd said, she lacked spite. Some would even call her innately kind. Despite reminding himself of the hell she'd put him through, he couldn't stop his gaze from travelling down the length of her body to take in the curve of her breasts, the flare of her hips, those long legs— and he found himself aching for a different kind of invitation.

He dragged his gaze back to her face to find her glass had frozen halfway to her lips, her eyes widening with a mixture of fascination and horror.

He snapped upright and slammed his drink to the bar, untouched. He needed to get out of here before he did something stupid. 'I know this is an odd request, but can you do the sketch tomorrow?'

She frowned. After pulling out her phone, she scrolled through what he guessed was her diary.

She shook her head. 'Not unless I've had a late cancellation…'

She clicked through a few buttons—probably her email—but eventually slipped the phone back into her purse with a shake of her head. 'I'm sorry, Lucas, tomorrow is impossible.'

He almost believed her sincere. She wouldn't work Sundays, but… 'Monday, then?'

'I can do Monday afternoon.' She hesitated. 'If you need this done quickly, I can make time on Sunday.'

He'd half turned away, but swung back. 'You will?'

She nodded.

Perhaps she wanted this over as much as he did? Except if she granted the request he'd come here to make, it would just be the beginning, and that thought left him exhausted. 'Thank you, Hallie. Sunday would be more convenient. What time?'

Straightening, she eased back a step and surveyed him. It left him prickling all over.

'I think we want to use the boldness of the full afternoon light. Two p.m. Do you need the address of my studio?'

'I have it already.'

'Excellent.' She didn't sound surprised.

He didn't offer her his hand. He didn't bend down to press a kiss to her cheek. He merely nodded. 'Until Sunday, then.'

Turning on his heel, he left. He fancied he could feel her gaze hot on his back all the way to the ballroom's grand double doors.

Hallie's studio was the top floor of an old warehouse in an inner-city suburb. There were windows on every wall flooding the space with light. A series of tables and shelving units, holding the tools of her trade, were assembled at one end of the room. The air smelled of paint and turpentine and...lemons? Which was when he noticed an oil burner flickering on the nearby window ledge.

This studio—it's situation and size—proved just how well Hallie had done for herself.

As if intuiting the direction of his thoughts, she said, 'It's a far cry from the old days when six of us shared that poky studio in Clerkenwell.'

'Yes.'

On Friday night she'd toasted his success, had even seemed to mean it. He should congratulate her on her own success, but he couldn't push the words out. It was petty. It was mean-spirited. And he loathed himself for it.

The raised eyebrow and the fleeting disappointment momentarily reflected in the opal-green depths of her eyes stung. But with a brisk clap of her hands, she became all business. 'Did you have any thoughts for how you'd like to pose?'

He didn't give two hoots about the damn sketch. He'd simply wanted two hours of her time. 'You're the expert. I'll leave the artistic decisions up to you.'

He flung the words out like a challenge.

Why? Why had he done that?

But it was too late to call them back.

In the bright afternoon sunlight her full lips twisted into the mockery of a smile. 'So you'd have no trouble if I was to tell you to remove your clothes?'

'I'm not posing nude for you!'

'You're not posing *for me*. I'm sketching a portrait you paid a hundred thousand dollars for.'

He'd posed nude for her in the past. And she'd painted him while not wearing a stitch herself. Quid pro quo. It had all been very egalitarian. And sexy. He did what he could to burn the memories from his brain.

She placed a straight-backed chair in a pool of light. 'I want you to straddle the chair like this.' She demonstrated what she meant. 'And I'd like you to look over there.' She pointed to the left.

Rising, she went over to a table and chose an object from among the ones scattered there. A cast-iron doorstop in the shape of…a chicken? Why hadn't she chosen the porcelain lady twirling in her big skirt, or the rearing horse or—?

'And you might want to take your jacket off. It's warm in the sun.' She gestured towards a hat stand where he could hang it, threw a cushion to the hard surface of the chair—a kindness he probably didn't deserve—before gathering her materials.

He straddled the chair, sans jacket, feeling oddly naked in his simple T-shirt. Gritting his teeth, he rested one clenched fist on the top of the chair and the other on his thigh, and glared at the blasted chook.

That chicken wouldn't be random. She'd have chosen it for a reason.

'Are you comfortable?'

His nostrils flared as he let out a controlled breath. He'd never been more uncomfortable in his life. 'Perfectly.'

The scratch of a pencil making lines on canvas sounded through the silence. He kept his eyes glued to the chicken, but felt the weight of her gaze when it rested on him. He clenched his fists harder, his back ramrod straight, and told himself he didn't care that she didn't try to make conversation. He vowed he wouldn't, either.

Was she frowning in concentration like she used to do? Was she remembering what it had been like the last time she'd sketched him? Could she see how much he'd aged in the past seven years?

Was she *bored* and counting down the minutes until his two hours were up?

He flicked a glance in her direction. She didn't

look up from her easel, but the top of her pencil pointed at the chicken. 'Eyes on the doorstop please.'

He did as she ordered. Her posture and expression had given nothing away. 'You once told me that making conversation to put a subject at their ease was a part of your job.'

The smallest pause sounded—the space of time it took to draw a breath. 'My apologies. I was under the impression you'd rather not converse.'

An impression he couldn't blame her for.

'I saw in this morning's paper that the shares for Rinngolt Holdings—' she named a technology company '—rose by a rather staggering one dollar twenty.'

She wanted to talk share prices? 'Are you looking for some free advice?'

Her chuckle held hard edges. 'Arsenal is doing well in the premier league. Some pundits claim they'll win the title this year.'

His lips twisted. She'd never liked football. 'I'm not getting my hopes up.'

'So I can see.'

He narrowed his eyes and imagined they were lasers, imagined incinerating that stupid doorstop chicken.

'I understand that Europe is on track for a glorious summer this year. Make me jealous and tell me where you're planning to holiday.'

It would depend on Enrico's health and what his doctors advised. 'I have no plans yet.' The words snapped out more sharply than he'd intended. In all likelihood it would be his grandfather's last summer, though, and that thought had a howl rising up at the very centre of him.

'Once upon a time you used to be obsessed with the stock market.'

'Obsessed? It was my job!'

'And you loved the football.'

These days football felt frivolous.

'And you dreamed of all the wonderful places you'd travel to when you were rich.'

For a moment that memory lightened something inside him, but the weight slammed back into place when he recalled why he'd abandoned those dreams. In each of them he'd always imagined Hallie would be by his side.

'It appears now, though, that they're of no interest to you. So I'm at a loss for what to chat to you about, Lucas.'

Her voice was oddly neutral and for some reason it made his stomach churn.

'I know there's a reason you're here, though you've not yet seen fit to inform me what it might be. And I don't feel like drawing it out of you like some precious secret that needs its hand held.'

He tried not to wince.

'So if you want conversation, how about you initiate it?'

He turned to face her. 'We both know this portrait is merely a pretext for me to see you. It's of no concern and—'

'Stop!'

She had at some point switched to paints and she held her palette tightly as if afraid she might fling it at him. She pointed the tip of her paintbrush in his direction. 'You paid a hundred thousand dollars for this portrait and I don't care if it kills us both. We're doing the portrait or I'm walking out of here. Your choice.'

Swearing under his breath, he glared at the chicken. 'Paint away! We don't need to talk. But if you could do this in under two hours, I'd appreciate it.'

'Noted.'

Sometime later—he had no idea how long, as he was too caught up in dark thoughts—Hallie told him he was free to relax. 'I'm just finishing up a few final details.'

He turned towards her, not wanting to draw this interview out longer than necessary. Her attention remained on the sketch. 'I'm here because of Enrico.'

'Your grandfather?' Her tone lightened. 'How is he?'

'Dying.'

Her quick intake of breath sounded through the air and he had to close his eyes.

'I'm sorry. I can't talk about this with any gentleness. I'm too angry about it, too...*angry*,' he repeated, probably sounding stupid. But Enrico's illness was tearing a hole in his world and he didn't know how to shore it up.

'Understood.'

Her tone was soft, but raw, too. He opened his eyes, but couldn't look at her.

'I'm sorry, Lucas.'

He nodded. Enrico had adored Hallie. And she him. 'He has asked of me a final request.'

'Which is?'

He met her gaze. 'He wants you to paint the Zaneri family portrait.'

CHAPTER TWO

BEHAVE LIKE AN ADULT.

Hallie very carefully set her paintbrush down, then tried to keep her expression neutral as she collected cheese from the little fridge she kept in the studio and set it out on a plate.

Paint the Zaneri family portrait?

She added dried apricots and dates to the plate.

Spend time with Lucas's family?

The foil packet of crackers rustled loud in the air as she shook a line of them around the plate's perimeter.

Spend time with Lucas?

Seeing him on Friday night and again today had shaken her, but it had also reinforced that she'd made the right decision seven years ago. It had let her catch a glimpse of the closure she hungered for.

It shocked her—the depths of Lucas's resentment towards her. Still. After all these years.

He'd always been driven, but had he also been this unforgiving?

Absolutely. He'd never forgiven his father. Why would he be any different with her?

The realisation started to shake something free inside her. This new vision of Lucas made it easier to imagine relegating his memory to the past, where it belonged. Like a historical tome that no longer held any significance and could now sit undisturbed on some forgotten shelf to gather dust.

She didn't want to be with someone who harboured grudges or refused to remember the positives. And to know her instincts seven years ago had been correct, that she hadn't made the biggest mistake of her life in walking away from him, was so damn freeing she wanted to weep with gratitude.

When Lucas had spoken about Enrico, though, she'd caught glimpses of the man who'd once meant the world to her. And her heart had trembled.

Staring across at the portrait she'd just painted, she let out a slow breath. No. She wasn't in danger of falling for him again. Not now.

'The silence is starting to feel oppressive.'

Lucas still straddled the chair, as if awaiting her permission to move, but those dark eyes watched her as if wanting to shake her thoughts from her head. Seizing the plate and two bottles of beer, she gestured to a table on the other side of the room.

He pointed towards the easel. 'Can I look?'

'Not yet.' At his raised eyebrow she added, 'It'll only distract us from the subject at hand. Though, if that's what you'd prefer—'

'No.'

She glanced at the easel and suppressed a sigh. He was going to hate the sketch. If she told him to go ahead and take a peek, he'd probably storm out of here and in all likelihood she'd never see him again. Problem solved.

Except Enrico deserved better. And she found herself unable to match Lucas's bitterness.

He joined her at the table, glanced at the beer. She shrugged. 'It's all I have. I can get you water if you prefer. It's low alcohol,' she added, in case he was worried about driving afterwards.

'The beer is fine.'

'Then why are you frowning?'

'Some things are very different.' He gestured at her studio. Lifting the bottle of beer, he angled its neck in her direction. 'And yet some things remain exactly the same.'

His words made her laugh, and the unexpected break in the tension had her breathing easier. 'I never did have champagne tastes. Fish and chips is still my favourite meal, I continue to drink beer from the bottle and I prefer curling up on the sofa with a good book rather than going to balls and dancing the night away.'

'Such a Cinderella,' he mocked, but a smile played around his lips, robbing them of any sting.

'Not when I have a castle like this,' she countered, toasting her studio.

He glanced around again and something in his eyes shuttered. Suppressing a sigh, she sliced off a wedge of Stilton and popped it into her mouth, letting the robust taste dominate her senses for a moment.

'Do eat something, Lucas.'

'Why?'

'Enrico once told me that some conversations were better had over a shared plate of food. So far, that advice hasn't led me astray.'

The tension in his shoulders eased a fraction. He reached for the brie. 'Sounds like something my grandfather would say.'

'And he wants *me* to paint the Zaneri family portrait?'

'He's watched the rise of your career with interest.' He shrugged. 'And pride. Your success has made him happy.'

'Unlike you.' The words slipped out and she wished she could haul them back.

He glanced across at her. 'That surprises you?'

What the hell; in for a penny... 'Sure it does.' She twisted the top off her beer, dropped the bottlecap to the table where it spun for a moment. 'Though it occurs to me now that I've probably projected my own generosity of spirit onto you.'

His head rocked back as if her words had connected with his cheek.

She sipped her beer. 'But we were never the same like that, were we?'

'It's not that I'm unhappy about your success. I never wanted you to crash and burn.'

Chanting *Liar, liar, pants on fire* would not be adult. 'But?'

He took a long drink, his eyes never leaving hers. 'It's just—' he set the bottle to the table again '—I prefer not to think about you at all.'

Which led to a whole new set of questions. 'So why are you even considering Enrico's request?'

'Because I care about him, and he's dying. I want to make him happy.'

She nibbled a dried apricot. 'You could've told him you'd asked me and that I'd refused.'

He shot to his feet. 'You can accuse me of a lack of generosity, but I'd never put what I wanted above my dying grandfather's wishes. If it makes him happy, then I care nothing for the trouble it causes me.'

She remained unfazed. If she led him across to the sketch, he'd leave and she'd never see him again. The thought was tempting. And it remained an option.

After slicing off another wedge of cheese,

she chose a broken fragment of cracker. 'So it's your sense of honour that brings you here?' She popped the cheese and cracker into her mouth.

He sat again, half glared half frowned, ate some cheese. 'If there's anything I can do to make his final months happier, I'll do it.'

Enrico only had months? Her eyes burned.

'I'm sorry I've not been friendlier, Hallie. I have zero desire to resurrect our past. My instincts tell me that you and I should remain on different paths.'

At least they were in agreement about that.

'But make no mistake. I want you to do this. I understand my request isn't a simple one given our history. But we're adults. Surely, we can act like it.'

She'd proven she could, but she was less certain about him.

'It's further complicated by Enrico's wish that you remain at the palazzo in Venice while you paint the portrait. I know,' he added when she jolted in protest. 'The time commitment he's asking is great, but he wishes to watch the portrait's evolution. Additionally, it isn't possible to get the entire family together at the same time.'

Ah. 'So different sections of the family would be sitting for me at different times?'

'Correct.'

It made sense. 'How many people altogether?'

'Eight.'

The more people, the harder the portrait. *And* she'd be working in oils. 'That would take me at least two months.'

'I'm well aware.'

So he'd done his research?

'You'd be compensated accordingly.' He named a sum that nearly made her choke. If he'd asked her to name her price she wouldn't have charged him half that amount. 'In addition, all of your living costs would be taken care of along with your travel costs.'

With all of his successes in recent years, money would be no object. Lucas could splash it about with gay abandon if he wanted to.

'Of course, time is of the essence. I will need you to come to Venice in the spring—April and May to be precise.'

It was February now...

'Will you do it, Hallie? Will you come to Venice and paint the portrait?'

Damn it. If it had been for anyone else but Enrico... 'Depends.'

'On?'

'Two things. The first is whether I can free up enough time in April and May to commit to it.'

Leaping up, she moved across to her desk and grabbed her diary, came back to the table and pulled her chair around so she sat beside him. He pushed the cheese plate to one side to make room for the A4-size diary. She opened it to a month-long view of April.

Glancing at her schedule, she pursed her lips. 'At this stage of my career I can't afford to alienate any big-name clients. They hold a lot of sway.'

He made an impatient sound in the back of his throat that she ignored.

'Anything in pencil can be rescheduled, but anything in black pen is something I've already committed to.'

He pointed to a couple of items early in the month penned in black.

She turned the page back to glance over her March commitments. 'I can have them finished early, before leaving for Venice, if I decide to accept your commission, but that—' she tapped a finger at an item later in the month '—might be a problem.'

She glanced up and met his gaze. He'd bent to stare at the page and it had drawn his face closer to hers. They shot away from each other at the same time. The pulse at the base of his throat pounded. Her heart gave a stupid kick. She might not like the man he'd become, but he was still devastatingly attractive. And she'd be a fool to forget it.

Reaching for a piece of Stilton and then taking a bite, she held it on her tongue, let it chase the smell of him from her senses. 'You'll be providing me with studio space, yes?'

'Yes.'

'So I can work on my other commissions while in Venice?'

'Of course.'

She turned the page to May, did some quick calculations. 'I might need to come back for a few days in the first week of May. But I could return to Venice immediately afterwards if your family can work around that.'

Firm lips pursed. She reached for the Stilton again.

'We'll have to make it work, I suppose.' He pointed. 'What does the green shading mean?'

He pointed to the last two weeks of May.

'Your timing is perfect.' He'd always been lucky like that. 'Those two weeks are supposed to be the annual leave I finally ordered myself to take this year for the first time in for ever.'

'Your…'

'I've deliberately kept my workload light in the weeks leading up to it.' She turned the page to display the following month. 'As you can see, that's more than made up for in June.'

He muttered something in Italian that sounded like a curse. One long finger tapped against the wooden tabletop. She'd always teased him about his hands, had told him they were the hands of an artist not a businessman. He'd always shot back with, *Business is an artform.*

'You'd give up your holiday for…?'

Him? She shook her head. 'Enrico is the dearest man alive. He was always very kind to me.' She'd do it for Enrico.

His gaze snapped away to stare out the window at the plane tree plush with summer green. 'He adored you.'

It had been mutual. It'd be good to see him again.

Lucas muttered another imprecation that had her eyebrows lifting.

'I need to warn you that there's more. He is...'

She leaned towards him, trying to decipher what lay behind the twist of his lips and the dark shadows that gathered in his eyes. Her fingers curled into her palms. Did Lucas mean that Enrico was emaciated? That he looked terribly ill and frail...was wasting away?

She rubbed a hand across her chest. Enrico was dying. He must be all of those things. 'Lucas?'

'He's playing matchmaker. That's what's behind this scheme of his to have you paint the family portrait. He'll say it's because he holds you in great esteem, that he believes you're the reason I found the family.'

Not to toot her own horn, but she was.

'But what he really wants is for you and me to reunite.'

Two opposing desires gripped her. The first was to laugh. *Oh, Enrico...* The idea was absurd. Oddly sweet and horribly naive, but utterly absurd. Lucas loathed her and she was never giving him that kind of power over her again.

She also wanted to cry. *This* is what caused the shadows in Lucas's eyes? How would he ever survive her being in his home for two whole months?

Hallie scrubbed a hand over her eyes and Lucas tried to catch each of the expressions that raced across her face. There was amusement mixed with sadness and affection. At a guess, he'd say Enrico was responsible for those. But it had been overtaken by something darker like disbelief and denial...or despair.

That last made no sense.

He forced his spine to straighten and focused on the hard seat beneath him. 'You said there were two conditions. We've established you *can* make the time. What other condition needs to be met before you agree?'

Chewing on her bottom lip, she stared at him before leaping up to pace between their table and the bank of long, low cupboards and shelves where she'd arranged this charmingly simple cheese plate.

Some conversations are better had over a shared plate of food.

He popped a date into his mouth and then held the plate out to her as she paced back. With a murmured, 'Thank you,' she sliced off some cheese and selected a cracker.

Even at her most absent-minded, Hallie never forgot her manners. Why couldn't he be like that? Scowling, he ate a slice of brie. And then another. Why did he have to be so tense and on edge? So full of snark?

If he'd needed further proof that she'd meant more to him then he had to her, he had it here. Seeing him had surprised her, shocked her even, but it hadn't turned her world upside down.

Not that he'd needed further proof. He'd known the moment she'd walked away from him. When she'd smashed his world—and his heart—to smithereens. In hindsight, he hadn't had a hope in hell of maintaining his equanimity when coming face-to-face with her again after so long. The only shock was that he'd found it so surprising.

He needed to recover his equilibrium now, though. If Hallie agreed to come to Venice, he needed to make one other request of her, and it was by no means a straightforward one. If she agreed to it, he'd need to dig deep. Far more would be demanded of him than a simple veneer of civility.

A part of him hoped she'd refuse and show him the door. A bigger and better part wanted the opposite. If anything he did now could bring Enrico happiness and peace then he'd do it.

He stared at the green shading in her diary. Her first holiday in for ever. He pressed his fingers to his eyes. Her footfalls against the wooden floorboards made soft padding noises as she continued to pace.

He dragged his hands from his face. 'Hallie!' Her name snapped from him with more force than he'd intended. *Equilibrium.* 'Would you kindly tell me what your other condition is?'

'Yes.' She halted. Though he had a feeling she spoke more to herself than to him. 'Would you like to see your portrait now?'

No. He wanted not to drag this out. He wanted to sort what needed sorting, fix what needed fixing, and then leave so he could breathe again.

He wanted to stop remembering what it had felt like to have her in his arms, to kiss her. He wanted the memories to stop trying to suffocate him.

Equilibrium. 'Very well.' He rose and followed her to the easel and the sketch she'd made of him. As he'd given her no guidelines, she'd chosen to do the sketch in oils.

One look, though, had a protest rising through him, gathering momentum like a fire in dry twigs. The sketch would take at least a day to dry, and it took all his strength not to reach out and drag his hand across the canvas to disfigure the likeness there. It was—

'That's...' There were no words awful enough.

'Masterful?' she supplied.

The word momentarily dragged him out of his fog. Hallie had always been remarkably talented, but in the past seven years she'd honed that talent. And the fact she could draw such a picture and create such an impact with so little extraneous detail was extraordinary. But...

'*That's* how you see me?' The words roared from him. So much for equilibrium. But the sketch was *hideous*.

She didn't flinch, as if his reaction hadn't taken her by surprise.

His nostrils flared. He flung an arm at the easel. 'You did that on purpose. To rile me—' to get under his skin and make him angry '—to punish me.'

Her eyes flashed. 'I sketched what I saw!'

He fell back at the expression in her eyes. Not anger. A bad taste coated his tongue. *Disappointment*. She stared at him with bitter disappointment. If it had been a colour it would be the deep blues and purples of a bruise.

Which is exactly how his insides had started to feel.

'I sketched what I saw,' she repeated. 'You refused to give me any kind of direction, and I gave you only the most basic ones—where to sit and where to look.' She gestured to the chair and the chicken.

His heart pounded too hard. That sketch made

him look ugly. Not physically—his body and face were almost godlike in their perfection—but in spirit. In her picture he simmered with rage, resentment, malcontent.

'You decided where to place your hands. You decided to clench them into fists.' She gestured to the sketch. 'You chose to scowl rather than smile, or look pensive or dreamy or relaxed or any of the million other things you could've chosen.' Her chin tilted. '*You* chose to thrust your jaw out like that. *You* chose to glare at Trevor as if you were trying to burn him alive.' She strode across to pick up the cast-iron doorstop and hug it as if trying to comfort it for the imagined injury.

'I didn't want the damn sketch done in the first place!'

'Then you should've sent me an email requesting a meeting rather than go through the machinations of bidding an outrageous sum of money on a two-hour portrait sketch at an auction,' she shot back with just as much fire.

A steel band wrapped around his chest. She was right. He'd gone through all of that rigmarole because he'd wanted to take her off guard, though he couldn't now explain why. Paying an outrageous sum for the sketch had been an attempt to make her feel beholden to him and, therefore, more inclined to agree to his request.

And while his appearance had shocked her,

it hadn't discomposed her. He hadn't succeeded there because he'd donned his ugliest face in an attempt to keep her at arm's length. And why? Because the thought of seeing her had left him raw and vulnerable.

And he didn't know how to say any of that without laying himself bare to her all over again. And *that* was the one thing it could never do. Not even for Enrico.

Swearing, he bent at the waist to rest his hands on his knees; drew in several deep breaths before rising again. She bounced that silly chicken in her arms like it was a baby and it had him huffing out a laugh. 'Why did you choose *Trevor* as my point of focus?'

One corner of her mouth twitched. 'I knew you'd overthink that.' Striding across to the table, she set Trevor down and picked up the porcelain lady in twirling skirts. 'I thought Clarissa here might remind you of Friday night at the gala—when you said that if you were polite you'd ask me to dance.'

Shame kicked him in the gut. Why hadn't he simply asked for a meeting? He could've had one of his PAs organise it.

'It seemed too pointed.' She set the twirling lady down, touched a hand to the rearing horse. 'Hector has far too much testosterone, and, let's face it, he's too phallic. I wasn't going there.'

He did his best not to let her words and the images they evoked affect him.

'These were too childish.' She lifted a couple of dolls that he hadn't noticed, before letting them flop back to the table. 'And this is too full of memories.'

She lifted a miniature painting in an ornate frame he'd bought for her birthday the first year they were together. It was a pretty landscape painted by an artist she'd admired. And seeing it now hurtled him back to the moment she'd unwrapped it. Her delight. The exuberant kiss she'd given him. A kiss that had developed into something far more sensual and—

'Way too many memories.'

He shook himself back into the present, his heart pounding hard.

'Which only left Trevor.' She patted the chicken on the head. 'I have a lot of affection for Trev. He makes me smile.'

She was right. He'd overthought it. There hadn't been anything nefarious in her choice. She'd in fact chosen something neutral that might've defused the tension if he'd let it, only he'd ignored the invitation.

He glanced back at the easel and tried not to flinch. She'd chosen Trevor because at least he'd made her smile. Nothing in that sketch could've done so.

She came to stand beside him, and the familiar scent of paint, turpentine and a hint of jasmine rose up around him. She folded her arms. 'Apparently, being near me makes you look like *that*.'

'What do you expect? Seven years ago you broke my heart.'

She stiffened.

'I wanted to remain on my guard.'

'I could counter with *you* broke *my* heart.'

'You're the one who walked away, not me.'

She pursed her lips and nodded, but it wasn't in agreement. 'You're not a "let bygones be bygones" kind of person, are you, Lucas.'

It was framed as a question but sounded more like a statement.

'Your resentment continues to burn just as brightly now as it did seven years ago. But you continually cast yourself in the role of victim, refusing to take any responsibility for your part in the breakdown of our relationship.'

She crossed to a window, her arms tightly folded and held close to her body. 'You never saw my side of things. Now I wonder if you were simply unable to.'

His role in their breakup? He clenched his hands so hard his entire body shook. 'I'd have done anything for you, Hallie. *Anything.*'

'That's not true, though, is it? The one thing I asked you for, you refused to give.'

At his blank look she added, 'Your time, Lucas. Your *time*.'

'You knew time was the one thing I was short of.' What little spare time he had he'd saved for her.

'Which proves that the assertion—that you'd have done anything for me—wasn't true.'

For God's sake. 'It wasn't a lie. You just had to be patient.'

'How long was I supposed to wait? You missed the opening night of my first exhibition. You knew how much that meant to me and—'

'I apologised for that.' He'd accompanied her the following night.

'You left me sitting alone at that fancy restaurant on the night of my birthday. You didn't even call to tell me you couldn't make it.'

The memory still shamed him. 'You know how sorry I was about that. You know—'

'Yes, yes, there was an emergency at work.'

She waved that away as if it was nothing. *Nothing?* It had been the kind of emergency that could've sunk his fledgling company. The company he'd created to secure his and Hallie's financial future.

'And then—'

She broke off. Swallowing a hard lump, he nodded. 'And I wasn't there when you miscarried,' he finished. He'd have given anything to have been in the country with her when that had happened, but he'd been in America chasing big-money investors.

She waved her hands in front of her face. 'What does any of it matter, now? Whether you'd been there or not, it wouldn't have stopped me from miscarrying.'

He'd been so busy setting up and consolidating Cormack and Quinn Holdings, while also preventing his newfound family's business from going into receivership. He'd spent all of his time feeling as if he was avoiding disaster by the narrowest of margins. *Every single day.*

But just for a moment he imagined what life would've been like if Hallie hadn't miscarried. If she hadn't left and they'd married, and now had a seven-year-old child—a little girl with the same strawberry blonde hair as Hallie and the same opal-green eyes.

Seven years ago, their unplanned pregnancy had felt like another weight to bear—one more thing to be responsible for. It was only once the baby was gone that the loss had hit him. 'I swore to you we'd try again. That there'd be children in our future.' If only she'd been patient.

Her chin lifted as if she'd read the condemnation in his face. 'How long was I supposed to wait, Lucas? You never would give me a time-frame.'

His heart beat too hard. Because he hadn't known the answer.

'Was I supposed to wait another year? Another three years? A lifetime? I saw myself turning into my mother and I didn't like it.'

His jaw clenched. He was *nothing* like her father. He'd have never asked her to wait for ever. And she knew it.

She gave a mirthless laugh. 'And here we are back at the same old impasse. I wanted your time and you wouldn't give it to me.'

'Couldn't,' he shot back.

'You chose to invest your time elsewhere, which you had every right to do.'

His mouth went dry.

'Just as I had every right to walk away if I couldn't live with the choice you made. *That's* what you refuse to acknowledge.'

He blinked.

After striding back to the painting, she surveyed it for a moment. 'If you can't put a better face on than that whenever I'm in the same room as you, you'll break Enrico's heart.'

And as the purpose of this entire enterprise was to make his grandfather happy...

He nodded, fighting exhaustion. 'You're right.'

She swung back, her eyes going as big and round as her palette board.

'I'm sorry, Hallie. I'm sorry I'm so angry.' The anger, though, had started to fade as soon as he'd mentioned the miscarriage. Replaced instead with loss. 'My anger is in large part due to my grief for Enrico.'

She chewed on her bottom lip. 'Okay.'

'Everything has changed in the blink of an eye.' He raked a hand through his hair and started to pace. 'And the thing is there is more I need to ask of you.'

She grimaced. 'More?'

'Enrico wants to see me settled before he dies.' The thought of Lucas spending the rest of his life alone caused Enrico pain, and of late, the older man had become more and more agitated about it. Lucas wanted his grandfather's last days to be peaceful ones, happy ones—joyful ones if it could be arranged. He didn't want him constrained by worries, fears or regrets. He did what he could to keep his expression neutral, but his lips twisted and a cramp started up beneath his breastbone. 'He's convinced you're my soulmate.'

Comprehension dawned in those remarkable green eyes and her jaw sagged. She pulled it back into place with a quick shake of her head. 'I'm not marrying you, Lucas. Not even for Enrico.'

'I'm not suggesting marriage.'

'What *are* you suggesting?'

Dragging in a breath, he straightened. 'It would give him much joy, but would also bring him peace, if he was to see us working our way back to each other.'

She blinked.

'Or thought that's what he was witnessing. In reality, we both know it's an impossibility. It's clear you've no more interest in resurrecting things between us than I have.'

Blowing out a breath, she stared doggedly at the portrait again.

'But if you do this thing for me—pretend to be falling in love with me again, perhaps even going so far as to become engaged to me, an engagement that will end when Enrico...'

He couldn't bear to say the word out loud and she gave a quick nod to let him know that she understood. He pulled himself back into straight lines. 'If you do that, then I will buy not just this studio but the entire building and have the deeds transferred into your name.'

CHAPTER THREE

HALLIE STARED AT Lucas and tried to work out how he could be so resentful, so unforgiving, and yet at the same time so *trusting*.

He gave a low laugh, totally lacking in mirth. 'I won't ever trust you with my heart again,' he said as if reading the thought in her face, 'but with all of my worldly possessions…' He shrugged. 'You've an innate sense of honour.' He gestured to the table where her diary still rested. 'Your horror at not delivering commissions when promised is proof of that. You're one of those rare people who, when they say they'll do something, deliver on their promise.'

He moved back to the portrait, surveyed it with hands on hips, his back ramrod straight. She tried to stop her gaze from lingering on the intriguing lines of that powerful body—the lean-hipped strength of the man. Unbidden, she recalled what it had been like to dig her fingers into the flesh of those hard buttocks, her body lifting up to meet his, and her fingers curled into her palms as her mouth went dry and her pulse haywire.

'It's also true that you're remarkably generous of spirit.'

Unlike him? The words hung on the air unsaid.

'Proof of that is in the fact you haven't thrown me out on my ear for behaving so badly.'

She recalled the way he could hold her on the edge of an orgasm until her body hummed and her mind had filled with him and she begged—

He glanced over his shoulder and she froze. Had she been caught gawking at him? His eyes narrowed and her mind blanked.

He turned more fully, frowning. 'Do you have anything stronger than beer? I know what I've just asked of you is strange, shocking even, and you're looking a little…stunned.'

She seized the lifeline he unknowingly handed her. 'Knocked sideways. Mind blown.' Stumbling back to her chair, she fell onto it, reached for her beer and took a careful sip. 'I don't need anything stronger, Lucas. I'm fine. I'm just trying to get my head around it all.'

Pretend to be in love with him again? Fake an engagement? Surely, that would be the height of folly—a stupid idea that could only end badly.

She drained the rest of her beer in one go. Or perhaps…not.

After having spent three years together—three

amazing years—it had all ended so abruptly. And so badly. She knew a large part of the reason she'd never been able to move on fully was because of her miscarriage. She'd woven so many dreams around that baby, and to lose it had broken something inside her.

She glanced across at Lucas. It had barely seemed to touch him. Yet, when he'd spoken of it earlier, she could've sworn grief had flashed through his eyes. Maybe the baby had meant more to him than he'd ever let on?

The thought bloomed across her heart like a bruise. She'd never been able to let go of the future she'd envisaged—her, Lucas and the baby a loving, happy family. Moving on had felt like a betrayal to the child she'd never had. She knew she shouldn't feel that way. And she knew it was time to move out from beneath that shadow.

Maybe spending time with Lucas, and keeping a record of all the reasons they'd have not suited in the long-term, would help her draw a line under that sad chapter?

Lucas dropped down into his chair, too. 'Hallie, it's far from principled of me to play on your heartstrings like this. But I remember how much you—' he hesitated '—loved Enrico. It's what gave me the courage to approach you.'

She stared at him, nodded. 'I did love Enrico.' She supposed a part of her still did.

When Enrico had learned of Lucas's existence and his connection to the Zaneri family, the older man had welcomed not just Lucas, but Hallie, as well, into the family with open arms and a joyful heart. She'd never experienced anything like it. It had felt like being wrapped in a warm cloud, a promise that she'd never feel alone again.

Enrico had made her feel a part of something bigger and stronger. His warmth and his kindness had made her feel cherished. She'd fallen in love with his wicked sense of humour, his strong principles and his zest for life. She'd wanted to emulate his boundless love for his family. She nodded. Yes. Enrico Zaneri was one of the dearest men she'd ever met.

'I should be above such manipulations, but…'

She glanced at Lucas again. But where Enrico was concerned, he'd do anything and everything to give the older man what he wanted. Exhaustion was etched into every drooping line of Lucas's body, his face ravaged with it, and her reluctant heart went out to him. It was an effort to keep her voice even. 'And if I agree to do… this, you'd buy this studio for me?'

He held up a finger. '*And* the rest of the building, don't forget. To sweeten the deal.' He flattened his hands on the table between them. 'And to keep things businesslike rather than personal between us.'

That was smart. If they each focused on what

they'd gain from this arrangement, it'd stop things from getting complicated or messy.

If.

Oh, stop it. She could do this. The man might be pretty to look at, but she had zero desire to start anything romantic with him again. She'd been down that path before. Never again.

But owning this studio—the entire building—would give her the financial security to launch herself on the European art scene. If she wanted to.

Oh, we're pretty sure you want to.

The world suddenly seemed to open up with new possibilities, and she could've wept at the relief of it. And if in agreeing to this it made an old man happy… 'What would it mean in practical terms?'

'We'd go on a few dates, look chummy when other people were around. Speak approvingly of each other to Enrico, perhaps? And when the time seems right, we could consider announcing a fake engagement.'

'And at the end of my two months in Venice?'

'If we're lucky enough to still have Enrico with us, then we embark on a fake long-distance engagement. Enrico will want to see us married, but we can insist on taking things slow. Maybe you and Enrico could have the occasional phone call or video call. I know it's asking a lot, but—'

'But this is a prime piece of real estate.' She

gestured around the studio. 'And what you're outlining doesn't seem to require that much effort.'

He leaned towards her. 'Are you saying you'll do it?'

She glanced at his portrait and back at him, raised an eyebrow.

He lifted both hands. 'You have my word that I will be polite and courteous at all times, not only when other people are watching.'

She wasn't sure why, but she believed him. 'Lucas, what's wrong with Enrico?'

He rubbed a hand over his face, but the shadows there remained behind when he pulled his hand away. 'Cancer. Stage four prostate cancer to be precise.'

Her stomach churned. 'That's… I'm sorry.' There weren't words adequate enough to do either her sorrow or her sympathy justice.

'He didn't have any symptoms for a long time.' His voice was low. 'And when he did, he put it down to old age. When he finally decided to get it checked out, it was too late. He's had radiation and has started hormone treatment. It will delay the inevitable but it won't cure him.'

'So…?' His gaze pinned her to the spot. 'Will you come to Venice? Will you paint my family's portrait? And will you pretend to fall in love with me?'

'On two more conditions. The first is that you

have a contract drawn up stating all this and only transferring the deeds of the building to me once we're done.' It would give her an out if for some reason she needed to walk away. 'And the other is I don't want to discuss the miscarriage.' She didn't have the heart or the strength for that.

CHAPTER FOUR

HALLIE'S STEPS FALTERED when her gaze landed on Lucas's tall figure in the Arrivals Hall, his dark hair gleaming beneath the lights. When she'd told him what time her flight landed in Venice, she hadn't expected him to meet her.

He hadn't seen her yet. His eyes searched the throng of people in front of her, though, and she was seized with an insane desire to dodge behind a pillar and hide.

Behave like an adult.

Gritting her teeth, she resisted the urge to duck down and sneak off to find a coffee cart. Instead, she fatalistically waited for his gaze to connect with hers. When it did, he stiffened. She could see him mentally—and physically—gird his loins.

Tell me again why you didn't hide until he'd gone away?

Because he wouldn't have gone away.

He lifted a hand in a wave, but didn't smile. She managed a smile, it seemed the polite thing to do, but her hands were too full to return the wave. As she drew closer, her pulse fluttered and flirted. With his dark hair, firm jaw and chiselled cheekbones, Lucas had the face of a Greek god. His height, the breadth of his shoulders, those long, strong legs, made him look like an athlete. He was the kind of man who stood out, and he—

Shocked her socks off when he bent down and kissed both her cheeks in the continental style! *'Buongiorno*, Hallie.'

Her pulse skipped and fluttered and behaved altogether badly. *'Buongiorno,'* she managed. The smoky notes of his scent threatened to surround her...to overwhelm her and hold her hostage. She shook herself. 'I'm, uh...surprised to see you.'

He halted in the act of taking her suitcase and hand luggage. She'd had all of her painting supplies sent on earlier in the week. However, as she was here in Venice for two months, that didn't mean she was travelling light today.

'Did I not promise you courtesy?'

He had. She just hadn't expected it to extend to picking her up from the airport.

'It made Enrico happy to know I was meeting you.'

Ah. 'How is he?'

'Surprisingly well at the moment, though he tires quickly.'

She'd need to be careful not to have the older man sit for her for too long. Sitting for any length of time in one position could be especially taxing.

As she followed Lucas out of the airport towards the car park, a sigh fluttered from her.

He spun around. 'Why the sigh?'

She stared at him, blinked. The old Lucas wouldn't have noticed, even if the sigh had been deliberately loud. He'd have been too busy pondering some tricky negotiation or business deal.

'I, uh… It doesn't matter.'

His frown deepened. 'You don't wish to share it with me?'

It was funny, but here in Venice he seemed more Italian than he ever had in London. Even though she'd known his father was Italian—a *depraved* Italian from all accounts.

And now this entire incident was in danger of being blown out of proportion. 'It's not that I don't want to tell you. It's just…' She blew out a breath. 'My original plan was to find a quiet corner and sip an espresso while waiting for the crowds to clear, before finding a water taxi. I realise, though, that you're a busy man and—'

'You never *liked* espresso.'

She could feel herself redden under his gaze. 'I've not had one since the last time I saw Enrico. I just wanted to…'

He raised an eyebrow.

'Practice keeping a straight face for when he insists on making me one.' She rolled her eyes. 'Because we all know I'll feel obliged to drink it.'

Dark eyes lit with amusement and those firm lips twitched into an actual smile.

She forced air into lungs that had forgotten how to work. At least if she flooded her system with caffeine she could blame her racing pulse on that.

'Airport coffee is not my favourite. I will take you to a place that makes the best espresso in all of Venice.'

What, *now*? She had to kick herself into action when he started walking again. Where was the Lucas she knew and what had this stranger done with him?

'*Sì?*' he asked, raising an eyebrow.

'*Sì,*' she agreed. 'Um… Thank you.'

His car was a sleek Italian sports car—because of course it was—and the buttery leather of the seat hugged her when she sank into it. Beauty, speed and comfort in one extraordinary and impressive package. With the international success of his company and the money he'd made, Lucas could afford to buy whatever his heart desired. Had the success and money made him as happy as he'd thought it would?

She'd love to know, but it wasn't a question she could ever ask. It was far too personal, and if she wanted this facade of courtesy to remain intact, she couldn't touch on subjects like that.

They were both quiet as he drove them to the facility where he garaged his car. Hallie couldn't stop her jaw from dropping at the sleek wooden speedboat moored outside, though—the polished wood gleaming in the sun, the pristine white leather interior screaming luxury.

One corner of his mouth hooked up. 'It's something, isn't it?'

'It's the most beautiful speedboat I've ever seen.' Not that she'd seen many.

That lopsided smile widened. 'It's my pride and joy.'

'So that…' She pointed behind them, indicating the garage.

'Is a consolation for whenever I have to leave Venice.'

She let him hand her into the boat. 'So you love it here in Venice, then?'

It was probably one of those terribly personal questions she shouldn't ask, but it didn't feel like a dangerous one.

He stowed her luggage, then turned back with a nod. 'It's home. I feel as if I've finally found a place where I belong.'

Her heart gave a painful twist. She'd once hoped he'd find that place with her. She plastered on a fierce smile. 'That's great.'

He started the motor and they set off across the lagoon. 'What about you?'

Mist hung in the air and Venice rose out of it in majestic lines, becoming clearer as they drew closer. She could see the square tower of the Campanile and the gothic domes of San Marco Basilica—familiar from a thousand pictures and photographs. A breath left her on a long, slow sigh.

'Is everything okay?'

She spared him the briefest of nods, before letting the view capture her attention again. 'Being here is like being in a fairy tale. I want to pinch myself to make sure I'm not dreaming.' She hadn't clapped eyes on Venice in over seven years, and she hadn't realised that something in her soul had hungered for this sight again. 'It's beautiful.'

Aware that she was in danger of waxing too lyrical, she dragged her mind back to Lucas's earlier question. Where did she consider home? 'My studio,' she finally said. 'I feel at home in my studio.'

'It's fortunate for me then that I landed on such an attractive bribe.'

Had he done that on purpose—mentioned the deal to keep it at the forefront of both their minds?

'That's not quite what I meant. I'm not refer-ring to any one particular studio. Once I have a space—any space—that feels right and that I can work in, I feel at home.'

The glance he slid across felt as if it was trying to take her measure. 'You're fortunate, then. It means you can take your home—or make your home—wherever you go.'

'Hypothetically speaking, absolutely.'

'And what does this hypothetical studio need to have to be *home*?'

Ah, now that could be hard to define. 'Lots of light is a good place to start, and I don't like clutter so if the space isn't large I'd want a storeroom. I also don't like being interrupted when I'm working or pulled out of the flow. Which is one of the things I love about my current studio. While there are shops below, the entire top floor is mine. I have no one walking by my door, accidentally distracting me.'

He didn't say anything.

'Of course, none of that is necessary as my shared space in Clerkenwell proved.'

'But your current studio indicates your level of success. That must be satisfying.'

'Absolutely.'

They grew quiet and she drank in the sights as Lucas negotiated his way along the Grand Canal, before turning down a smaller side canal. Clasping her hands beneath her chin, she admired the tall buildings on either side—some in the Gothic Venetian style, others in the Classic style. Some painted in pastel colours, others looking run-down, but in a picturesquely atmospheric way that nowhere else on earth could make look half so romantic.

Lucas pulled into a mooring. 'It's captivating, is it not?'

Utterly. 'It's so grand, and I want to say charming, though the word feels too twee for all of this.'

After stepping from the boat, he held out a hand and she placed hers in it, grateful to hold on to something steady as the boat rocked. He didn't release her immediately, glancing around instead. 'Venice has a timelessness, a strength and yet also a fragility.'

All true, but she couldn't focus on his words. An odd music thrummed to life in her veins at his touch. Heat gathered beneath her breastbone.

For the briefest of moments he smiled down at her, like he used to do back when their hearts hadn't been broken, and she stood there frozen as if in a time warp.

But then he blinked, and while the smile remained on his lips, it faded from his eyes. He dropped her hand. 'The *caffetteria* is just along here.'

He led her down a side street and turned in at an unassuming shopfront. Inside the shop was narrow but long, and the scent of coffee filled her lungs in an invigorating rush.

'If you choose a table, I'll order the coffee.'

He hesitated, raised an eyebrow. 'You're sure you want…?'

'An espresso? Yes, please.'

She chose a table with a view of the fresco on the wall opposite. She didn't know the legend it depicted, though she'd bet Lucas did. If the conversation lagged, she'd use it to kick-start it again. In fact, why wait? She could ask him the minute he sat down and keep the conversation pleasantly impersonal.

Before she could, though, he said, 'I'm glad you wanted coffee,' before planting himself in the seat opposite.

She tried to stop her brows from shooting up towards her hairline. Even given his courteous facade, she doubted he wanted to spend more time in her company than necessary.

Though maybe he wanted the practise. So he could be convincing in front of his family.

'I've been wanting to apologise. I behaved abominably five weeks ago.'

'Lucas—'

'I was angry and bitter, and I took it all out on you. I love Enrico, as you know, but I felt manipulated by him, too.'

The grooves on either side of his mouth deepened and her heart burned. He'd felt trapped. And like a wild animal caught in a trap, he'd lashed out. 'You're grieving for him. You're being inundated with *all* the emotions. It's understandable.'

He stared at his hands, though *glared* might be more accurate. 'If we're going to pull off this charade convincingly, I expect I need to be honest with you.'

She wrinkled her nose. 'Maybe not too honest, though.' She didn't want him stating in words of two syllables or less exactly what he thought of her.

Her words surprised a laugh from him, dispelling some of the tension that had wrapped around them.

'The fact is, Hallie, when we broke up seven years ago, I boxed up my feelings for you and buried them. Seeing you again had them rushing to the surface. It caught me off guard. I wasn't prepared for it.'

An ache stretched through her chest. She hadn't meant to hurt him so badly. She'd never wanted that.

He smoothed his face into tidy lines. 'I was ugly to you and I'm sorry. You were right in all that you said to me. I wanted to blame you for everything without acknowledging that I, too, was at fault. I hope you'll accept my apology.'

Their coffees arrived and she waited until the server moved away. 'Apology accepted. I accepted it back in Australia.'

'Thank you.' But the tension in his shoulders didn't ease.

'I hope you know I never wanted to hurt you.'

He nodded. 'Nor I you.'

The difference, though, is that she'd always known that whereas even now she could see he didn't believe her.

'You have my word that from now on I'll do my very best to only present you with my better self.'

She couldn't have said why, but that felt like a loss. And it was going on her list. The two of them could now never again be natural or unguarded with one another. It was awful.

'While we're here I should probably fill you in on a few things. But first, come…try your coffee.'

Lifting the tiny cup to her lips, she inhaled the heavenly scent before taking a careful sip. It took all her strength to stop her face from screwing up in revulsion.

He took a sip of his coffee, his eyes not leaving her face.

Steeling herself, she took another sip, but with a grimace and a shudder, abandoned it back to its saucer. 'God, Lucas, how can you drink this stuff? It smells like heaven but tastes vile.'

With a low laugh, he gestured to the server and a beautifully frothy cappuccino appeared in front of her with maddening speed.

Lifting it to her lips, she closed her eyes and savoured the creamy goodness. When she opened them again, she found Lucas watching. For the briefest of moments she could've sworn she'd surmised hunger in his eyes.

She had to be mistaken. Despite his apology, Lucas would never trust her again. He might have changed in the past seven years, but he wouldn't have changed that much.

The dreamy appreciation that raced across Hallie's face at her first sip of cappuccino, recalled to mind other times her face had suffused with pleasure, and the memories arrowed straight to Lucas's groin. He had to stare into the dark depths of his espresso and silently recite his eight times multiplication table to find his balance again.

This *wanting* was inconvenient, but it wasn't Hallie's fault. She'd been a lot of things, but manipulative wasn't one of them. She wasn't trying to seduce him. She had no idea he still found her attractive, and he had every intention of keeping it that way.

His shoulders started to ache from how tightly he held them. He needed to find a way to stop being so *emotional*. He needed to find the ragged scraps of his reserve and wrap them tightly around himself, make himself impregnable again.

In Australia he hadn't been able to hold back the bitter rush of memories, the crushing pain, the anger. His eyes had lasered in on her at the charity gala in a heartbeat, as if she were a magnet. She'd stood there sparkling among a roomful of people, her dress clinging to her every curve, her hair falling around her shoulders in strawberry blonde waves, her lips full and inviting—and a howl had started up at the centre of him. The force of it had knocked him off his axis. It had overwhelmed him, turning him into a growling beast of a man. He who was usually so controlled!

He'd let himself down. That *wouldn't* happen again.

Clenching his jaw, he recited his nine times table. It *couldn't* happen again. Not if he wanted to pull off this charade. Not if he wanted to convince Enrico that he and Hallie were working their way back to one another.

'What things do you need to fill me in on?'

Her words pulled him back into the present moment. 'Everyone thinks that you and I have been enjoying an email correspondence for the last five weeks.'

She nodded. 'Roger. Got it.'

'You've been enjoying the glorious weather in Australia and getting to the beach as often as you can.'

Her soft laugh had things inside him unclenching. 'Some things never change. And as both of those things are true it will be easy to play along with.'

'Also, your last client—' he named an Australian rockstar with an international reputation '—was delighted with her portrait.'

Her jaw dropped. 'Do you know her?'

It was his turn to laugh. 'No, but her name was in your diary. And as your paintings are extraordinary, it's a foregone conclusion that she loved it.'

Her mouth worked but no sound came out.

He shrugged. 'You congratulated me on my success and it's my turn to congratulate you. I've done some research, have seen photographs of your portraits. They're extraordinary.'

Her eyes went so wide he was worried she'd strain an eye muscle. But then she blinked and drew in a breath and seemed to gather herself again. 'I…thank you. And, yes, my last client was very pleased with the finished product. It's always a relief. And a joy. Now, tell me who *everyone* refers to. Clearly, we're performing for more than just Enrico.'

Did she mind? He briefly wondered what had ultimately won her cooperation for his scheme. Was it her affection for Enrico? Or the ownership of the studio? Perhaps she felt guilty for all that had happened in the past and wanted to make amends?

Did it matter? And did he care as long as they succeeded? '*Everyone* refers to my immediate family—Enrico, my aunt Francesca and her partner Chiara, my aunt Rosa and her Juliet.'

All of whom she'd met.

'Got it.'

'Fran and Chiara live in a nearby apartment, but Enrico, Rosa and Juliet all live at the palazzo.'

She glanced up. 'They live with you? How did that come about? I mean, I remember how unhappy Enrico was that he'd had to sell the family home, but his apartment was very grand.'

The selling of the house that had been in the family for generations had happened two years before Lucas had met the family. Lucas had tried to make up for its loss by creating another family home where they would always be welcome.

'And I notice you haven't mentioned Marco.'

He shrugged, finding himself strangely reluctant to talk about the family with her.

'In the ordinary course of events, I wouldn't ask, Lucas. But if we've been chatting away for the last five weeks then these are things I should probably know.'

Her wince speared into the centre of him. He shouldn't be making her feel guilty for asking such questions. 'You have every right to ask about such things. You're right. You should know more. You're doing me a favour.'

Their gazes caught and clung. Something

arced between them, but then she pulled herself back, leaning away from him and staring down at her coffee. 'Not a favour, a business deal, remember?'

Her words washed over him like ice water. A business deal; that was what this was. And he'd be a fool to forget it. All that was required of him was to fill her in on the necessary background information—coolly, efficiently and without drama.

You also need to pretend you're falling in love with her.

He ignored that. He'd work on it later.

'Rosa and Marco divorced. It was amicable enough and Juliet sees her father regularly.'

'Okay.'

'I also came to realise how lonely Enrico was in his big apartment on his own, so I badgered him to move in with me. I had more room than I knew what to do with.' And if the truth be told, Lucas had been lonely, too. 'At around the same time, Rosa and Marco were having marital difficulties. It just made sense for everyone to move in with me.'

She smiled then, and there was nothing cool or efficient or detached about it. 'And you found yourself suddenly surrounded by family and loving it.'

He had.

'It's wonderful that you can give them a home, Lucas.'

Of all his accomplishments, it was the one of which he was most proud, the one that meant the most to him.

They finished their coffees, but before he could rise and lead her back to the boat, she said, 'Can I ask you something?'

She'd caught her bottom lip between her teeth, nibbled at it. He did his best not to notice. 'Okay.'

'Has Enrico…'

He leaned towards her, raised his eyebrows.

'Has he changed much?' she blurted out.

He let out a slow breath. 'You're worried his illness has changed him?'

'I'd like to be prepared.'

Her voice was low and something in it caught at him. 'He's lost a little weight and he doesn't have his old energy.' He ran a hand through his hair. 'But he still has the same twinkle in his eyes. He still has the same sense of humour.'

That brought a smile to her lips. 'And he still loves his family with the same fervour he always did.'

Which brought a smile to his. 'Very much so. You don't need to worry, Hallie. You will recognise him.'

'I'm sorry I asked. I just didn't want to look shocked if he was much changed.'

'There's nothing to apologise for. Now come, he'll be impatient to see you.'

They arrived at the palazzo twenty minutes later. Hallie's eyes went gratifyingly wide as she took it in. '*This* is your home?'

He stared at the handsome facade that rose in front of them in four imposing floors, and satisfaction rippled through him. 'It was run-down when I bought it. I got it for a song.' Not entirely true. 'I had it fully restored and renovated.'

'How old is it?'

'It was originally built in the seventeenth century.'

'No way,' she breathed as he handed her out of the speedboat and led her inside the huge entrance hall.

'Back then this area would've been the warehouse. The original owners were merchants—they dealt in wine, spices, carpets.' The space was now an entertaining area for when they had parties. 'Come.' He gestured towards the staircase. 'The living areas are on the next floor.'

He'd grown used to the grand rooms with their plush furnishings, though when he'd first moved in he'd sometimes had to pinch himself. This was the antithesis of the poverty he'd grown up in. He tried to see it through Hallie's eyes now.

Catching his gaze, she grinned. 'It's beautiful. It suits you.'

There was no rancour or envy in her face, no

consternation. He'd once dreamed of her seeing all of this and gnashing her teeth in frustration and regret because it could've been hers, too. He scrubbed a hand over his face. He should've been above that, been a better man. He *would* be that better man.

Rosa came rushing through from the kitchen with a wide smile, seventeen-year-old Juliet trailing behind wearing a sulky expression.

'Hallie!' Rosa embraced her. 'It is lovely to see you. We are so excited to have you here. Papà is delighted beyond measure.'

'Oh, Rosa, it's wonderful to see you, too.' Hallie clasped his aunt's hands, her smile a sudden beacon of brightness that squeezed his heart tight.

'You remember my daughter Juliet?'

Hallie's eyes widened. '*This* is little Juliet?'

Hallie took a step towards the teenager, but with a scowl, Juliet stepped back. Hallie's smile faltered, but only for a moment. 'My, how you've grown, Juliet. It's lovely to see you again.'

Juliet's scowl deepened. 'Not mutual,' she muttered.

'*Juliet!*' Rosa's jaw dropped.

'I don't see why I have to pretend to be happy to see—' she waved a disparaging hand in Hallie's direction '—*her*.'

'Hear, hear!' Fran said, coming in from the next room, and Lucas had to suppress a groan.

Francesca was the elder of his aunts and had been far from thrilled when she'd learned Hallie was to paint the family portrait. 'Why should any of us be delighted to see this woman again?'

'Fran, that is appallingly rude!' Rosa's eyes widened and her lips firmed.

Fran simply shrugged. 'I thought it rude that she broke my nephew's heart.'

Rosa groaned.

Juliet folded her arms and nodded. 'Exactly!'

Grabbing her in a friendly headlock, Lucas ruffled her hair, making her squeal and laugh. 'What do you know about it, *mostriciattolo*?' Little monster.

Rosa turned back to Hallie. 'Do not listen to either of them. We're delighted to have you here.'

'And even if we're not,' Lucas inserted smoothly, releasing Juliet, 'everyone will be polite and courteous.'

'But—'

'No buts,' he said over Juliet's protests, fixing Fran with what he hoped was a glare. 'Don't forget that if it wasn't for Hallie, I would never have met any of you.'

'Enrico!'

He turned at Hallie's voice, watched her race across the room to the doorway where Enrico stood. As soon as she reached him, the older man embraced her, kissed both her cheeks and then held her at arm's length. '*Bellissima!* You are a sight for sore eyes. My old heart, it beats harder just seeing you.'

Hallie laughed, her hands firmly ensconced in the older man's. 'You always were an incorrigible flirt, Enrico.'

'You have made an old man very happy.'

'Old, my foot! *You?* You have a heart that will remain young for ever.'

He chuckled at her flattery, and something in Lucas's chest lightened. Bringing Hallie here had been the right thing to do.

'Is my family giving you a hard time, *cara*?'

'Do you doubt my ability to hold my own?'

'Not for a moment.'

'Especially not when I have a white knight.' She gestured to Lucas.

Lucas did his best not to fidget beneath their combined stares.

Enrico's eyes brightened. 'Yes?'

'Absolutely.'

Lucas couldn't help but smile at how easily she'd changed the direction of Enrico's thoughts into happier channels. Her lack of drama. Her easiness. He appreciated all of it. He also appreciated how natural she made it seem for Lucas actually to be her white knight.

'Now, as much as I would like to sit down and sip espresso with you and catch up on all of your news, alas, I cannot. There is a doctor coming to see me.' He rolled his eyes. 'There are always doctors.'

'Then perhaps we can share a pot of tea later and catch up properly.'

The older man laughed, clapped his hands. 'Some things do not change, I see. We will debate your choice of beverage later.'

When Enrico had left, Lucas turned back to Fran and Juliet. He needed to make it clear that he expected them to extend every courtesy to Hallie while she was here; but before he could, Hallie slid her hand into the crook of his elbow. 'I'd be grateful if you could show me to my room, Lucas, and tell me where I might find a bathroom.'

'Of course.'

He led her from the room and as soon as they were out of sight, she released him. He led her up the next flight of stairs to the third floor. 'You don't want me to take Fran and Juliet to task for their rudeness?'

'They're your family, Lucas. They love you. They only have your best interests at heart. It's nice of them to be protective of you. Give them a chance to adjust to my being here.'

Maybe she was right. But the thought of anyone being rude or discourteous to her on his watch chafed through him. She'd rearranged her entire timetable to do this crazy thing for him.

The least he could do in return was ensure her comfort.

She's not doing it as a favour. At the end of all this she'll have a prime piece of Sydney real estate.

And yet, he knew that there was some sentiment involved, too. Besides, she'd put up with enough rudeness from him to last a lifetime. He wouldn't let his family add to it as well.

CHAPTER FIVE

'How would you like the family members arranged, Enrico? Have you given that any thought?'

Hallie and six members of the Zaneri family stood in the formal drawing room of Lucas's palazzo, an array of furniture at their disposal.

'I do not wish everyone to be sitting in lines like they are posing for a school photograph,' the older man said. 'Your British royal family does portraits nicely, I think.'

Hers? That made her smile. Due to the fact that she and Lucas had met in London, and Lucas had lived in England for much of his life, Enrico considered her British, too. As Australia was part of the Commonwealth, though, technically the British royal family *was* hers.

Behind her, Fran snorted. As if nothing associated with Hallie could possibly be nice. It was shaping up to be a long afternoon.

'I thought, *cara*, you would have an idea of what might work best.'

Fran snorted again. This time with impatience.

'Papà, we should commission Giuseppe de Mosta to paint our portrait. His work is celebrated internationally.'

'Hallie's will be one day, too. But that reminds me…' Enrico turned towards his grandson. 'Lucas, I promised Hallie that you would arrange an introduction to Giuseppe for her.'

What the heck? Her startled glance met Lucas's and he sent her the smallest of nods to acknowledge his recognition of Enrico's machinations. She dragged her gaze away. Oddly rocked that they could still silently communicate with such ease. *That* wouldn't make it onto her list of reasons for why she and Lucas shouldn't be together.

'I'll see what I can arrange,' Lucas told the older man.

Fran gave a loud huff and Lucas's eyes snapped a warning.

'I also wish to arrange tickets for you and Hallie for opening night of *La Traviata*. It is playing at Teatro la Fenice in a few weeks. Lucas, can you believe Hallie has never been to the opera? *Cara*, you will be spellbound. There is nothing like the Venetian opera.'

'That is not necessary, Nonno. I will arrange the tickets myself.' Lucas shot a smile in Hallie's direction. 'You must experience the opera at least once while you're here, Hallie. It's magical.'

Juliet shot Hallie the kind of glare that only

teenage girls could manage. Yep, a *very* long afternoon.

'I'll look forward to it. In the meantime, back to the task at hand,' she said, clapping her hands. 'In terms of the arrangement, we can consider several options. I'll take photos and you can decide which one you like best. But let's start with placing you, Enrico. We want you at the centre of the portrait.' In a *comfortable* chair.

She went to move a plush wingback chair into the centre of the space, but Lucas was there before her. 'Where would you like it?'

He wore a short-sleeve polo shirt and they'd both bent forward at the same time, which meant there was nothing but thin air between her and the flexing rope of muscles in his forearms. Swallowing, she pointed to where she wanted the chair placed.

Not noticing. Definitely not noticing.

Turning to Enrico, she found the old man surveying her; a knowing smile hovered about his mouth. She shrugged and sent him an abashed grin, pretended to herself that the surreptitious ogling had been a deliberate ploy, that it was all for show.

She gestured for him to take the seat. 'Lucas tells me there'll be eight people in the portrait altogether.'

'There or thereabouts.'

There or thereabouts? Hmm… She raised an

eyebrow. Enrico gazed back with an innocence she didn't trust. What was he up to?

None of your business.

'Let's have your daughters either side of you. One sitting and the other standing.'

'I'll stand,' Rosa said. 'I have the younger legs. Fran can rest her weary older bones.'

'Cheeky,' Fran said, but there was a smile in her voice. There was only two years between the two women.

'I'm not sitting on the floor like some child.' Juliet folded her arms and stuck out a hip.

'No, no, *cara*,' her grandfather assured her. 'I want you standing with your mother, holding your violin.'

Hallie glanced at the teenager. A violin?

'She plays beautifully,' Rosa said. 'She's aiming for a spot in the Venetian orchestra.'

'How very exciting.'

The teenager did her best to look unmoved. 'Do I need to get my violin?'

It wasn't necessary, but she suspected Juliet would welcome a short time-out, so she nodded. 'Good idea.'

'And I want Fran holding her needlework frame. And for Lucas to stand here just behind my shoulder.'

They all moved into position—Fran's wife, Chiara, standing behind her.

Hallie tapped a finger to her chin. 'And we're

missing Enzo and Matteo.' Fran and Chiara's two sons were away at university in Rome, but would return during the semester break. 'One can stand beside Chiara and one can sit beside Fran.'

She went to pull another chair into the tableau, but found Lucas once again at her side insisting on moving the furniture for her, quietly solicitous and flooding her senses with his scent—a mix of amber and spice, leather and salt. It was more invigorating than caffeine.

When everything was arranged, she gave directions to all of those present before snapping a picture on her tablet and handing it to the older man. 'Here's one option.' She leaned across and pointed. 'Enzo would be here and Matteo here.'

'It is perfect!'

'Another option would be—'

'No, no, *this* is what I want.' He tapped a finger to the tablet. 'It is exactly what I imagined. Thank you, Hallie. You are a genius.'

Fran rolled her eyes. Juliet curled her lip. Rosa beamed. But it was Lucas's swift glance of approbation that settled in her bones like a throb. *It's just for show.* She smiled back. *That* was just for show, too.

'Lucas,' Enrico said, handing him Hallie's tablet, 'can you email that to everyone? I love the directions Hallie gave for how we should all sit and stand, where to look and our expressions. Everyone must memorise them.'

She bit back a smile at his autocratic directive.

'Now, Hallie, would you be kind enough to lend me your arm and lead me to my sitting room and take coffee with me?'

'I'd love to.' She promptly offered him her arm. 'As long as you make mine a cappuccino and *not* an espresso.'

He laughed. 'Very well.'

A short time later they were seated in his generous sitting room with its balcony doors flung wide open to the canal below.

'I wish to ask of you a favour, Hallie.'

She set her cup down, giving him her full attention. 'Which is?'

'I am dying.'

'And you know how very sorry I am, Enrico.'

They'd had this conversation yesterday. It had been decreed that Hallie should spend her first day in Venice settling in while Lucas spent it working. *Of course.*

She'd enjoyed a catch-up with Enrico in the afternoon, though, and had even managed to slip into the conversation what a pleasure it had been to see Lucas again after all of these years. He'd beamed and clapped his hands, *so* delighted. In that moment she'd seen why Lucas's resistance had crumbled, and why he'd undertaken to enlist her cooperation for this hare-brained charade.

Enrico gave a soft chuckle now. 'Do not fear. My mind doesn't wander. I just wish to impress upon you how important this favour is to me.'

'Okay.'

'I want to see my son. And I want you to paint him into the portrait.'

She tried to stop her jaw from crashing to the floor. *'Massimo?'*

Enrico and his son had been estranged for many years. Massimo's rebellious and irresponsible ways had created a rift between him and the rest of the family when he'd been a young man of twenty. That rift had widened when Lucas had introduced himself to the family eight years ago. Enrico and the rest of the family hadn't known that Massimo had fathered a child thirty-four years ago. Or that he'd refused to acknowledge the infant as his own. Enrico had been furious on both counts. But now he wanted...

'You want to see Massimo? And you want me to *paint* him into the portrait?'

He nodded and stared at her for a long moment. 'That is not all I'm asking of you.'

Oh, God. 'You want *me* to find him for you?'

'Who better?' He spread his hands. 'You found us all of those years ago for Lucas, did you not? You have a talent for these things.'

No, she didn't! She'd just happened to get lucky. Lucas's birth certificate had given her Massimo's full name, and she'd known the dates that Nicola's ballet company had toured Venice. After that it had been a simple matter of elimination.

With her own mother long since dead, Hallie didn't have any family other than her father—a workaholic who was totally uninterested in his daughter and who rarely noticed either her presence or her absence. She'd hungered for a large extended family and couldn't believe that Lucas had zero interest in tracking down his own, despite his protestations otherwise. She'd put his resistance down to a sense of loyalty to his late mother whom he'd worshipped.

Both he and Nicola had tarred the wider Zaneri family with the same brush as Massimo— had expected them to display the same selfish and cold indifference. But in this instance Hallie had been vindicated. The Zaneri family had welcomed Lucas with arms wide open.

Massimo, though, was an altogether different proposition. He'd turned his back on his son and on the young woman who'd believed him when he'd told her he loved her. He'd behaved reprehensibly. She completely understood Lucas's aversion to ever meeting him.

'Enrico—'

'And when you find him, I want you to tell him that I am dying, that I wish to see him, and I want you to convince him to sit for you so he can appear in the portrait.'

Her mouth dried.

'But nobody else in the family must know of this.'

'You want me to lie to Lucas?' Her heart plummeted.

Lucas would never forgive her once he found out. And they'd all find out at the unveiling of the portrait. Her stomach churned as she imagined his reaction. He hated his father. *Hated* him. Held him responsible for the fact that he and his mother had lived in poverty; held him responsible for his mother's death, for the fact she hadn't been able to afford the treatment that might've saved her life.

The entire family had shed bitter tears when they'd heard that story. If she was to meet with Massimo behind Lucas's back... Dear Lord, he'd feel betrayed a second time. And he'd *never* forgive that.

She moistened her lips. 'Enrico...'

'You are not yet a parent.' The older man's face had gone haggard and her heart went out to him. 'I am not saying I approve of the things Massimo has done or of the way he has lived his life, but he is still my son and I love him. I cannot help it.'

She rubbed a hand over her face.

'And it does not seem too much for me to ask to see him one more time. *Please*, Hallie.'

A lump lodged in her throat. 'Enrico, I can't lie to Lucas. Not about this.'

The older man's shoulders slumped.

'It would be too unkind. It would hurt him too badly. If you give me leave to tell Lucas—'

'*No!* I do not want other opinions colouring this. I do not want the fuss. I just…' A breath shuddered out of him. 'Please promise to think about it, to at least consider it before you refuse a dying man a final wish. I am begging it of you.'

'Enrico—'

'You refuse my grandfather a dying wish?'

She swung around to find Lucas in the doorway, his mouth working and his eyes wide and betrayed. As if he'd unknowingly smuggled a serpent into his Venetian Garden of Eden. Then a shield slammed down into place and he stared at her like she was something that had crawled out of a drain.

For a moment she felt as if she'd been punched in the stomach. The two of them had a deal, but he clearly didn't expect her to keep it. She folded her arms tightly across her chest. *Of course* in his eyes she'd have to be the one in the wrong in this scenario, rather than Enrico. Not that she had any intention of disabusing him of that notion and landing Enrico in hot water instead.

Always to blame. That was *so* going on her list. As was his inability to trust her even after she'd given her word.

Her list was growing at a gratifyingly rapid rate.

Clenching her jaw, she ground down the furious words that burned the back of her throat, reminding herself of what she'd promised to do here. Summoning an image of her studio to mind, and then imagining glorious success on the European art scene, she tried to find a sense of detachment, a sense of purpose. Her gaze drifted to Enrico, whose hands twisted in his lap, and her eyes burned. *Oh, Enrico.*

Dragging in a breath, she met Lucas's gaze and tried to send him a silent message. 'Lucas—'

'Don't!' His face twisted. 'This was a mistake—a big mistake. I'm sorry, Nonno, we should never have invited Hallie here. She's changed. She's someone I now no longer know.'

'Don't be such an idiot,' she snapped. Couldn't he see how much Enrico enjoyed having her here, and how his hopes that they'd get back together sustained him? Lucas might think she was being unkind to his much beloved grandfather, but at least give her the courtesy of hearing her out!

'An idiot?' His mouth worked. 'An idiot!' His face twisted and his eyes glittered. 'I was wrong about you. I thought you generous hearted. What a joke! You don't *have* a heart.'

'A total idiot,' she shot back, nearly losing hold of the threads of her temper and exploding like a red-hot lava ball. 'There's a perfectly simple explanation if you'd only stop to listen to it!'

He slammed his hands to his hips. 'Fine.' His lips turned thin and white. 'I'm all ears.'

Dimly, she was aware of Enrico's head going back and forth between them as if he was at a tennis match.

'What's this *perfectly simple explanation*?'

She moistened suddenly dry lips. Um…excellent question. 'Well… I um…'

Cynicism twisted his lips, but it was the revulsion that darkened his eyes that left her feeling bruised and aching all over. She clenched her hands so hard she started to shake. 'What's the deal with you these days anyway, Lucas? Don't you have something better to do…like work?' He always had seven years ago. Work had been more important than anything. Including her miscarriage! 'Instead of sneaking around spying on me?'

'Not spying.' He thrust her tablet at her. 'I thought you might need this.' His nostrils flared and he gestured towards his grandfather. 'Is your refusal some sort of punishment directed towards me?'

'Don't be ridiculous! *I'd* never be so petty.'

He leaned towards her, his eyes blazing. 'I don't believe you.'

She slammed her hands to her hips, her every

pulse point pounding. 'I don't care what you think, you pompous—'

'Enough!' Enrico gave a loud clap of his hands.

Hallie swore silently. She'd made a promise to herself not to lose her cool around Lucas, to behave like an adult.

Big fail.

Damn it all to hell, she was supposed to be pretending to fall in love with Lucas.

Bigger fail.

Thank you, Captain Obvious!

All of the emotions she'd tried to contain since the night of the gala dinner in February had simmered to the surface as if they'd been on the boil for a *very* long time. With one disparaging glance, Lucas had released them. She was putting that on her list, too, though she didn't know what she was going to call it. Other than infuriating.

Actually, rather than just keeping that list on her phone, she was going to make a hard copy. This afternoon. She wanted to have that list nearby *always* as a reminder and an antidote to the infuriating attraction that burned deep inside her. Where Lucas was concerned, she couldn't afford any weakening or softening; she couldn't let herself imagine for a moment what it would be like to give in to temptation. Enrico started to chuckle. 'Oh, watching the pair of you, it makes me feel young again.'

She froze.

'To be so passionate.' Enrico pressed his hands to his heart and gave a happy sigh.

Passionate? What she and Lucas felt for each other wasn't passion. It was anger and mistrust and—

Oh, God. She covered her face as if in embarrassment at Enrico's words, but really, she just wanted to hide from him and all that he'd read into her and Lucas's heated exchange. Because there was an element of truth in it and it frightened her to the marrow of her bones.

'To be so feisty and full of indignation and lust, so full of righteousness and outrage...' He trailed off with a shake of his head. 'I miss it. I do, but with age comes a different balance. With age comes wisdom.'

She pulled her hands away and lifted her chin. The older man chuckled at whatever he saw in her face, as if she'd delighted him. From the corner of her eye she saw Lucas frown.

'You do not think me very wise in the request I just made of you, though, do you, *cara*?'

She deflated on a sigh. 'It's not the request itself that I take issue with.'

You are not yet a parent. Tears burned her eyes. No, but she'd hoped to be. Once. Seven years ago.

She couldn't give his secret away. It wasn't her place to, but… 'I think I understand the impulse behind your request. I think I would likely feel the same.'

Taking the seat beside him, she reached for his hands. 'But as I explained, it's the execution I have an issue with.'

'You do not wish to lie.' The older man squeezed her hands, then glanced up at his grandson. 'You are wrong, Lucas. Hallie's heart is not hard. Her heart is pure.'

Enrico released her hands. 'I will take your advice then, Hallie.' He thrust out his jaw. 'If I tell Lucas the truth, will you do this thing for me?'

Oh, God. It would gut Lucas. *Gut him.* And despite all the anger still swirling through her, she didn't wish this upon him. Not for a second.

She couldn't speak for the lump that lodged in her throat. She nodded instead.

Lucas glanced at Hallie and then Enrico, trying to read the undercurrents threading between them. Hallie briefly met his gaze, those opal eyes swimming with something that looked like concern.

Concern for Enrico? For herself? He swallowed. Or for *him*?

The thought had a harsh laugh scraping from his throat. For all of her so-called good behaviour—acting mature and above the bitterness that had overpowered him—the sudden flash of her temper had left him feeling scorched.

And oddly satisfied, which made no sense.

'No, no, my boy.' Enrico shook his head. 'You misread Hallie's motives. She refused my request because she did not wish to lie to you.'

He froze. Her *idiot* echoed through his mind. Had he misread the situation? Jumped to conclusions?

'She did not wish to hurt you.'

Not a sentiment that had stopped her in the past.

His mouth went dry all the same. His heart started to thud. 'Why would she believe anything you requested of her would hurt me?'

Enrico rubbed a hand across his eyes, looking suddenly old. 'Because in this instance she would be correct, dear heart, though I wish it were otherwise. The fact is, Lucas, I wish to see Massimo.'

He took an unsteady step backwards. Enrico wanted to see Massimo? After everything the other man had done? The ground beneath his feet rocked. He widened his stance to keep his balance. *'Massimo?'* He spat out his father's name.

'The request I just made of Hallie was to ask if she would find him and approach him on my behalf.'

Massimo had deserted Lucas's mother, Nicola, when she'd become pregnant, had refused to help her financially after she'd given birth to their infant son, even though he'd had the means. Massimo had deliberately turned his back on them, had sentenced them to a life of poverty and hardship. Nicola Quinn might still be alive if Massimo had acted differently.

But he hadn't and Lucas would never forgive him for that. And Enrico wanted *to see him*?

Ice encased him. He turned to Hallie. 'I apologise for misreading your motives. It was unfair and unkind of me. I hope you'll forgive me.' The words sounded as if they came from a long way away. Without another word he turned and strode from the room.

It wasn't until he reached the stairs that he realised Hallie was behind him. Seizing his arm, she tugged him up the stairs to her studio on the fourth floor. His mind whirled with too much confusion to offer resistance. Everything inside him throbbed.

When she let go of his arm, he paced around the room, the violence of his thoughts needing a physical outlet. Instead of trying to make sense of the confusion, he focused on his surroundings. 'Do you like your studio?' He growled the words in her direction.

He'd tried to create the studio of her dreams. It wasn't as big as her studio in Sydney, but the large windows at either end of the room flooded the space with light. The south-facing French windows led out to a tiny balcony that had a view of the canal below, while the north-facing windows looked out over the surrounding roof-tops. The high ceilings gave the space a sense of vastness. It felt like an eyrie.

When she didn't immediately answer, he turned to find her moving towards a pair of wingback chairs—the kind of chairs that he knew she loved and called Alice chairs because they were like the one the Mad Hatter from *Alice in Wonderland* had sat in. She carried two bottles of beer in one hand and a bowl of potato crisps in the other. She set them to the round table between the chairs.

'I don't *like* this studio, Lucas. I *love* it.'

Her words were a balm, soothing the agitation chafing through him.

Folding herself down into the nearest chair, she crossed one shapely leg over the other. 'It's as if you took everything I ever said I wanted in a studio and rolled into one and came up with something that exceeded all my expectations. I mean *Alice chairs*! It will be a joy to work here. Thank you.'

She reached into the bowl and then lifted a crisp to her mouth and crunched it, her eyes half closing in… Not appreciation, but an odd relish.

Glancing up, she caught his gaze and stopped

midchew, shrugged. 'When I was a kid I used to clench my jaw in my sleep. I'd wake up in the mornings with a sore jaw and neck. My mother started making me eat an apple half an hour before bedtime. Apparently, the crunching and chewing gives jaw muscles a workout and gets them to relax. Which is probably why I find crunching potato chips so satisfying now whenever I'm stressed.' She gestured to the bowl. 'Help yourself.'

He strode over and took a handful, crunching several as he continued across to the windows with the view of the rooftops at the other end of the room. He turned back with a glare. 'They're not helping.'

She lifted her gaze from a notepad where she was furiously jotting something down. 'Had to add something to my list before I forgot,' she murmured, pushing the notebook down the seat beside her, then lifting her beer to her lips and taking a long drink. For a brief moment, his mind flooded with forbidden images. *That* didn't improve his temper, either.

'Crunch two more.'

He did as she ordered.

'Seriously?' She pointed her beer at him. 'Are you honestly saying that crunch isn't the tiniest bit satisfying?'

Grumbling, he strode back and threw himself

down into the other Alice chair, seized another handful of chips, drank some beer.

'Enrico said something interesting to me,' she eventually said, and with a start he realised the silence that had stretched between them had been oddly comfortable, even companionable. Soothing. No way was he letting himself get used to that. 'He told me that I was not yet a parent. Which is true enough. It's true for you, too, yes?'

'Of course!' It shocked him she even had to ask.

'Don't look at me like that. I know you'd never abandon a child of yours, but it's possible for you to have a son or daughter that I didn't know about.'

When he and Hallie had been together he'd never thought about having children, hadn't known if he'd wanted them or not. Until she'd blurted out one evening that she was pregnant. Even then he still hadn't known. And before he'd been able to work it out, she'd miscarried. He stared at his hands. The baby hadn't felt real until it was gone. But once it was gone, it had left a gaping hole at the centre of his heart that nothing else had been able to fill.

'And because you and I aren't parents, Lucas, we can't truly understand the love a parent has for their child.'

The things that had been soothed by their silence started to burn once more.

'I think parents love unconditionally.'

His lips twisted. 'Some parents.' Massimo wasn't of their number.

'Parents like your mother,' she said. 'And Enrico. He's a family man through and through— caring, kind, protective—and it's clear how much he loves all of you.'

Lucas rested his elbows on his knees, his beer dangling from his fingers. He mightn't have been lucky in his father, but his mother had loved him with her whole heart. Nicola Quinn had been a dancer, on tour in Italy with her ballet company when she'd met Massimo. And so young, just twenty-one. Massimo had swept her off her feet, had promised her the world, but had promptly abandoned her when she'd told him she was expecting his baby.

She'd started dancing professionally at the age of seventeen, hadn't graduated high school, and when an injury ended her career she'd had few resources to fall back on—her own parents having died in a car accident a couple of years earlier. But she'd had boundless energy and had worked hard to create a good life for herself and her son. They'd lived in a council flat in one of Lancaster's less salubrious neighbourhoods. She'd cleaned houses and took in ironing to make the rent and keep food in their bellies.

While Massimo had continued to live the high life. Lucas's hands clenched at the unfairness of it.

'I don't think you should take Enrico's desire to see Massimo as a reflection of the love he has for you.'

He met her gaze.

'We can love people without liking them. Enrico will never approve of the way Massimo abandoned you and your mother. The fact he wants to see him doesn't mean he's reconciled to the way Massimo has lived his life or the decisions he's made. But now that he's dying, I think it's a natural impulse to want to see him one more time. But it isn't a reflection on you... or on Fran or Rosa. They'll be no happier with this news than you are. But it doesn't mean he loves you any less.'

Her words made sense, though they couldn't erase the feeling of betrayal he'd experienced when Enrico had told him what he'd asked Hallie to do. 'It won't bring him joy.' Which wasn't a thought that brought him any satisfaction, either.

'I don't think Enrico is looking for joy. I think he just needs to say goodbye.'

The red glow of her hair caught the light, haloing her in rose gold. He dragged in a breath. 'You refused...?'

'To go behind your back?' She wrinkled her nose. 'I didn't want Enrico lying to you about it—and, therefore, making me lie about it, too.' She picked at the label on her beer, peeling it off and creating a tiny pile of paper on her knee. 'Our history is fraught enough. I knew how you'd feel about me searching for Massimo behind your back. I didn't want to add that to the tally of crimes against me.'

He would have blamed her, too. It wouldn't have been fair, but it would've been easier to blame her and her influence than to blame Enrico. So much for the level-headed rationality he'd been trying to cultivate. He rubbed a hand over his face. 'I nearly blew everything.'

She held a finger and thumb a centimetre apart. 'This close.'

When he'd thought she'd been denying his grandfather his request as a way to punish *him*, he'd lost his mind. He'd thought he'd made a major miscalculation, that in bringing Hallie to Venice he'd done something that would cause Enrico great pain rather than joy. 'I'm sorry for jumping to conclusions.'

'So you said.'

She had every right to throw his apology back in his face. She'd never given him any reason to believe that she could be so callous. He needed to stop being so suspicious. He needed to stop being so emotional.

'I hope in time I can find a way to make it up to you.'

'You already are, Lucas. You're gifting me not just my studio but the entire building, remember?'

Her words made him want to wince, though he didn't know why. She clearly didn't want to talk about his abominable behaviour any further so the least he could do was let it drop. 'You said something about the truth coming out?'

She gathered up her little pile of paper and set it on the table. 'He wants me to paint Massimo into the portrait.'

He couldn't have stopped his jaw from dropping if someone had held a gun to his head.

Glancing up, she grimaced. 'And in the interests of not whitewashing your family's history, I agree with him.'

She what?

'No matter how much we want to, we can't change the past, and it's an undeniable fact that Enrico has three children. Enrico isn't interested in leaving behind a *pretty* family portrait, Lucas. He wants me to capture a true picture for the generations to come.'

She *applauded* him for that?

Rising, she moved across to her easel. He followed to find a preliminary sketch of the portrait there. She pointed to a spot away from the gathered family group. 'I think I'll place him here. Maybe with his back to the rest of the family.'

Some stiffness in him eased. *That* suited him fine. *And* was true to life.

'If I can get him to agree to sit for me, that is.'

She turned and he had to ease back a step, unaware he'd drawn so close. Blinking, she backed up, coughed and swallowed. 'That's supposing I can find Massimo in the first place. Enrico thinks I'm some kind of whizz because I tracked him down all of those years ago.'

For the first time in a long time, it hit him how much he had to thank this woman for. If it hadn't been for her, he'd have never bothered trying to track down the Italian side of his family. He'd been too bitter at the father who'd abandoned him to think anything but ill of the rest of the family.

He'd inherited his mother's mistrust of the Zaneris. When he'd wanted to know more about them, she'd told him she would find them for him if that was what he wanted. But he'd sensed her reluctance and had shaken his head. He'd not wanted her to suffer any further rejection or humiliation on his behalf. He'd put that family out of his mind. Until Hallie.

If she hadn't started digging, hadn't shown him the newspaper reports that detailed a public rift between Massimo and the rest of his family, and had helped him overcome his reluctance, he'd have never met the family who'd come to mean so much to him. The thought now seemed inconceivable.

He raked a hand through his hair and pulled in an unsteady breath. 'What do you think I should do?'

Her head rocked back. 'Is that a trick question?'

'No.' He forced the words from his throat. 'You were always better at this stuff than me.'

'You should talk to Enrico, that's what.' She pointed a bossy finger at him. 'You need to make things right between the two of you.'

He shouldn't have walked out like he had. The older man would be beside himself with worry.

His hands clenched and unclenched. He also needed to overcome the resentfulness inside him and be a better person. Enrico deserved that and so did Hallie. Regardless of what her reasons might be—whether they were sentimental or material—she was helping him. 'Do you think…? What if I offered to help you track Massimo down?' She shouldn't have to do that on her own. 'If Enrico wishes me to keep my distance, I'll understand, but…'

Reaching out, she made as if to touch his arm, but her hand dropped back to her side before it made contact. 'I think he'll be delighted by the offer.'

Then she moved away to tidy up their empty bottles of beer and the potato chips.

Her words had soothed something inside him, though he suspected he'd done nothing to deserve it. Blowing out a breath, he forced himself to say, 'Hallie, you've been incredibly generous. I...thank you.'

She finally turned, planted her hands on her hips. 'We need to be more careful. We've got away with arguing like that once, but any more...'

He nodded.

'Now, go away, I want to work.'

He couldn't explain why, but her exasperation made him smile. 'Hallie?'

She glanced up.

'I mean it,' he said. 'Thank you.'

CHAPTER SIX

A GENEROUS COURTYARD meandered at the back of the palazzo with an impressive fountain at its centre. A tall fence and iron gate shielded it from passers-by on the street. Established trees and pots of colourful flowers had turned it into an oasis—serene and inviting. A variety of benches beckoned, offering sanctuary.

It'd be the perfect spot to retreat with a cup of tea and a good book. Something Hallie was planning to do this very weekend. Setting her mug in the sink, she stared out the kitchen window planning which spot she'd choose. Either the bench over there by the pot of geraniums, or—

Or the one Lucas currently sat on. Correction. *Sagged* on.

Watching him had an ache blooming to life in her chest. With elbows on his knees and head in his hands, he looked wretched and dejected. As if the world had become too heavy for him.

She'd only ever seen him look like this once before—the night she'd left seven years ago.

She folded her arms, tightly wrapping her fingers around them, and reminded herself that she wasn't the cause of his current pain. That culprit, no doubt, was Enrico's desire to see Massimo.

As soon as Lucas introduced himself to the Zaneri family, they'd embraced him with wholehearted zeal—welcoming him with a deep and innate affection that had made him feel like an integral part of the family. In return, he'd given them all of himself, all of his heart.

She suspected he'd wanted to make up for the bitter disappointment Massimo had been to them. And as recompense, too, for not daring to seek them out sooner. He might've indicated yesterday that he'd reconciled himself to Enrico's desire to see Massimo, but that didn't mean it hadn't hurt him, that it hadn't shaken his world or that he didn't feel betrayed by the grandfather he looked up to.

He wouldn't appreciate her intrusion on his reflections now, though, or—

A movement on the balcony above had her gaze lifting. Enrico stared down at Lucas, his hands pulling at his hair. He looked as if he might burst into tears.

From the opposite side of the courtyard, in one of the upper rooms, music started to blare—rock music. Probably from Juliet's bedroom. The girl was obsessed with music. She glanced from Lucas to Enrico, caught her bottom lip between her teeth. Maybe…?

Not giving herself time to think, she strode out to the courtyard, careful to keep her gaze from straying upwards. 'Lucas, there's something I've been meaning to tell you.'

She planted her hands on her hips and hitched up her chin in deliberate challenge. His head lifted, and when his eyes rested on her they darkened. As if a part of him still wanted her, desired her, craved her.

A pulse ticked to life deep inside her. Gritting her teeth, she maintained her defiant stance. She and Lucas were supposed to be convincing Enrico that they were falling in love again. Lucas was gifting her prime real estate to help him do that. She'd known when she'd agreed to this that she might need to dig deep on occasion. And this, clearly, was one of those occasions.

Lucas rose, but remained silent. Ignoring the warnings that rang through her mind, she forced herself forward until she stood less than a foot away. She pointed a finger at his chest. At his very *nice* chest. 'The thing is I *can* dance now. I took lessons. I expect I can now jive, waltz, quickstep and cha-cha-cha as well as you.'

That was a bald lie. Lucas's mother had been a dancer and she'd taught Lucas to dance before he was even able to walk. Dancing was in his blood. But she should at least be able to hold her own these days.

Perfectly sculpted brows rose. 'You want to dance with me?'

She hitched her chin higher. 'I'm simply challenging you to a dance-off.' Sotto voce, she added, 'Don't look up but Enrico is watching. He's clearly worried about you so play along.'

Swearing under his breath, he took her in his arms and waltzed her around the perimeter of the courtyard. Engulfed by his warmth and his scent, she did what she could to keep her lungs functioning—*breathe in, breathe out; rinse and repeat*.

His lips unconsciously relaxed—not into a smile, but as if the movement and the music eased something inside him—and things inside her clenched up tight. Staring at that firm, sensual mouth had her remembering...*too many things*. But mostly how, when Lucas had kissed her, he'd made her feel as if she was at the centre of the universe.

'Do you wish me to also kiss you?' he murmured, but the derision that laced his words doused her as effectively as if he'd thrown her into the canal.

'No, thank you.' She dragged her gaze from his mouth and tossed her hair. 'But switch it up, Lucas. The waltz is boring and—'

Before she'd finished the sentence, he'd spun

her out the length of his arm and back again, before leading her into a quickstep. Thank God it wasn't the rumba. She'd forgotten about the rumba—the dance of love. That wasn't a dance for her and Lucas. Not any more.

Besides, he wouldn't. He wouldn't want to dance the rumba with her.

He made the quickstep deliberately quick and she was glad of it. It helped to keep her mind on her feet and the steps rather than the enticing heat he gave off. A heat she was horrified to find that she yearned to surrender to.

How he'd laugh if he knew. What derision would be poured over her head then!

'Enrico?' he muttered through a clenched jaw.

She flicked a glance upwards through her eyelashes. 'Smiling,' she murmured back. The older man also silently clapped in time to the music, but she didn't tell him that bit. Meeting those stormy eyes again, she found it impossible to look away.

'Can we stop yet?' he ground out.

No way; not until the song ended. She might regret having started this fiasco, but for Enrico's benefit she'd see it through to the end. 'Falling in love, remember?' She sent Lucas her sweetest smile. 'We can stop when the music does.'

He effortlessly transitioned them into a cha-cha-cha.

If you'd said yes, this torture could be at an end now.

Shut up.

His frown became a scowl. 'You *can* dance.'

He said it as if accusing her of something dastardly like theft or fraud. 'Told you so.' She only just prevented herself from sticking out her tongue. *So mature.*

'And who, I wonder, taught you to dance?'

His nostrils flared and so did hers. He made it sound *sleazy.*

'Oh, that's right!' She pressed the back of her hand to her brow like some swooning lady. 'You were going to teach me to dance. In all your spare time. Of which, if I remember correctly, you had none.' Placing her hand back on his shoulder, she matched him glare for glare. 'I can't imagine you're too disappointed about missing that chance.'

The music had finished, but Lucas kept whirling her around as if trying to wrong-foot her. As if the dance had become a battle. She gritted her teeth. He'd need to try harder. A new song started. Sparks flew from their eyes, and she imagined that they flew from their feet as well.

'Your teacher was a good one.'

She could barely keep up with him, but he was also a very good partner. He wanted to put her through her paces, punish her for starting this, perhaps, but he wouldn't let her come to any harm.

His chin took on an arrogant tilt that had her mouth drying. It shouldn't be sexy. It *shouldn't* be.

'But I'm a better one.' And then he transitioned them into a slow and sultry rumba to suit the slower pop song—a love song.

Her every instinct told her to wrest herself out of his arms and run. She didn't want to dance *this* dance with *him*. It was too provocative. But to flee now would be to admit defeat. And that was out of the question.

So when he moved with a flagrant masculine possessiveness, she angled her hips and chest towards him and mirrored his movements, undulating her hips with an equally flagrant feminine sensuality. She gasped when one strong thigh slipped between her legs, nudging her in *places*. That move hadn't been in any of the lessons she'd taken!

Fine, if he could improvise and make moves up…

She arched her breasts and throat in a silent invitation that made his eyes darken. The dance was a dark, teasing temptation that made her ache and unleashed a deep craving in her blood.

And despite the derision he could inject into his voice, and the scorn he could fire at her from his eyes, she could see that he wanted her, too.

With the same hunger he always had. The fire between them when they were younger had been exciting, a revelation, a delight.

Now, though, it was all anger, antipathy, grief. It could bring neither of them anything but pain.

And pleasure, a little voice whispered through her. So much pleasure.

The movement of the dance brought their bodies close; their hips touched, and they stuttered to a halt. The music flowed all around them, their chests rising and falling from their exertions, their eyes locked.

That heated gaze roved over her face. Things inside her melted and yielded. The gaze fixed on her lips and she imagined that mouth following, imagined firm lips moving over hers…the kiss deepening—

With a cry, she tugged her hand from his, and he released her immediately, took a step back. Not wanting to see the mask of derision descend over his face, she turned on her heel and made for the living room.

'See?' she tossed over her shoulder. 'Told you I could dance.'

She applauded herself for the flippancy of her delivery, but halfway across the thankfully empty living room, Lucas caught up with her. Unrelenting fingers gripped her elbow and urged her up the stairs to the fourth floor and her studio. She could've tugged herself free, but he was right—they needed to talk about what had just happened.

Like mature adults.

She had to make sure nothing like that ever happened again. She wasn't falling under Lucas Quinn's spell a second time. *Once* was enough.

He slammed the door shut behind them. 'What the hell was that? Were you deliberately trying to seduce me?' He glared as if the idea was the stupidest he'd ever heard, and the last thread of her control snapped.

'If I was trying to seduce you we'd be in bed already!'

So much for maturity.

'You—'

She spun around, advanced on him, her finger making stabbing motions in the air, her face twisting. 'Do you seriously think I would *ever* risk becoming pregnant by you again? Not a chance, Lucas. Not *ever*.'

It felt as if her words had sucked all of the air from the room. He paled, the grooves beside his mouth deepening.

'I saw the look on your face when I told you I was pregnant.' She wheeled away. 'And when I miscarried, the one thing you weren't was gutted. I will *never* put myself through that again.' She didn't have the emotional resources to go through that again.

She swung back. 'You storm back into my life

making sure I'm *very* aware that the last thing you're interested in is a reunion, not realising I'm every bit as opposed to that idea as you. What possessed you to think I ever would be?'

In the pallor of his face, his eyes throbbed.

'Ha!' She whirled away, hating herself for the knives she'd flung at him, tried to pull her agitated emotions back under control. 'So no. Seduction was the last thing on my mind.'

She paced across the room, concentrated on her breathing. 'But once again you go off half-cocked, reading something nefarious into my motives.' Turning back, she folded her arms. 'Humour me. Remind me what it is we're trying to achieve here?'

'To convince Enrico we're falling in love.' His eyes flashed. 'But there's a line that can't be crossed and—'

'And if I told you he'd been standing on the balcony above the courtyard staring down at you, literally pulling his hair out at your—'

His lips whitened. 'My...?'

Sadness. Despair. 'You looked as if you were carrying the weight of the world on your shoulders.'

Closing his eyes, he swore.

'You needed brisking up while he needed his mind eased.' Finding a space amid all her painting paraphernalia, she leaned back against the cabinet, stretching along one wall. 'I was actually doing the job you're *paying* me to do. I thought challenging you to dance would lighten the moment and show him that our "relationship—"' she made quote marks in the air '—was developing.'

Some of the colour returned to his cheeks. 'That dance crossed a line.'

She pointed a surprisingly steady finger at him. 'And that's just as much your fault as mine, so don't go hurling all of your resentment at me.'

He blinked.

'Neither of us want to feel—' she searched for a word that wouldn't inflame the situation '—anything for the other. But given our past history, that's probably not a realistic expectation, is it?'

Had he really thought seeing her every day would be easy?

Had she?

She sure as hell hadn't thought it'd be this hard!

Lucas wanted to yell and stomp and fling his arms out, but he'd behaved badly enough for one day. It was just… Having Hallie in his arms again had brought the memories crashing back.

He'd dated since they'd broken up, but nobody had stuck. Nobody had made him feel like Hallie had. Nobody had sent him scaling those same heights. After Hallie had left, he'd locked his heart behind impenetrable walls, resolved to never suffer that kind of pain again. So the fact he'd never fully connected with someone else romantically was, in part, his own fault. How did he expect anyone to stick when he kept himself so out of reach and inaccessible?

But a single dance with Hallie had him craving what they'd once had. He'd been tempted to throw caution to the wind. It had taken a superhuman effort to keep his head and not drag her up to his bedroom and make love with her until neither of them could think straight—until they felt replete and whole again.

That was a lie, though, an illusion. It would merely be a temporary panacea. Hallie would leave again when her two-month tenure here was up, and if he let his guard down he'd be every bit as devastated as he'd been seven years ago.

Way to go, Lucas.

His weakness for this woman appalled him. And in his frustration and his rage at himself, he'd lashed out at her.

Straightening, he forced his gaze to meet hers. 'I'm sorry for losing my temper. And for being so stupid. You've no more reason than me to wish for a reunion in earnest. I can't believe I considered anything so patently ridiculous.'

Trusting this woman did not come easily, but she cared about Enrico. He couldn't let himself forget that.

*Do you seriously think I would ever risk be-
coming pregnant by you again?*

Her words replayed through his mind and he
tried not to flinch. The miscarriage had devastated him as much as it had her, and something
inside him broke at the thought that she'd never
realised that. While the pregnancy hadn't been
planned, it didn't mean he hadn't welcomed it.

He'd just been juggling so many balls at the
time. He'd needed to work out how a baby would
fit into their lives, had needed to work out how
to add *father* to the growing list of roles he'd
taken on—CEO, fiancé, business partner, new-
est member of the Zaneri family. He'd felt overwhelmed, apprehensive that he wouldn't be able
to do justice to any one of those roles let alone
all of them. He'd needed time to adjust.

But then the miscarriage had happened and
the baby was gone and all that had been left behind had been a gaping hole. He'd felt as if he'd
given too little too late and had been punished
for it.

Hallie, naturally, had been devastated. He'd
focused on comforting her, on being strong for
her. The one thing he hadn't wanted to do was
add his grief to the burden she already carried.
It hadn't been *her* job to make *him* feel better.
But none of that had meant he hadn't cared about
the baby or hadn't mourned its loss.

He opened his mouth to tell her as much, but

closed it again. The words she'd flung at him had been hasty, said in the heat of the moment, but back in Sydney, she'd made it clear that the miscarriage was a taboo topic—it had been a condition of her agreeing to come to Venice. A condition he'd agreed to. He'd given his word. He didn't want her storming out of here never to return. Not when Enrico had gained a new lease on life with her being here.

Besides, what was the point in digging up the past and reliving old pain? It wouldn't change anything.

He fell down into one of the Alice chairs. It might not change the past, but one thing he sorely needed to do was let go of his anger and bitterness. That old revenge fantasy of his—the one where he bumped into Hallie and she, discovering how successful and wealthy he now was, regretted walking away from him with every atom of her being—had been nothing more than a mirage.

His lips twisted. On her part he'd imagined teeth gnashing and the tearing of hair while he'd been completely indifferent, utterly emotionless. But the opposite was true. She had zero interest in him while he was the one gnashing his teeth.

What the hell kind of man had he become? He hadn't known he could *dislike* himself so intensely. It had to stop. He needed to start being his better self. Not just for Hallie's sake, but for his own, too. He couldn't explain it, but it felt as if he'd lose himself if he didn't start acting like a better person around her—*being* a better person.

Since their breakup, he'd wanted to write her off as someone who had no ability to weather the hard times, someone with no stamina or endurance, but the fact of the matter was she'd never realised how much he'd loved their baby. She suspected he hadn't loved it at all. And she loathed him for it.

'And you're doing it again.'

Shaking himself, he glanced up.

'Falling into the doldrums,' she said, chewing on her bottom lip. 'Look, I know how conflicted you must be about this thing with Massimo.'

She thought his doldrums were about Massimo rather than the baby they'd lost? He opened his mouth. *Leave the past where it belongs.* He closed it again, dragged in a deep breath. 'I'm not *conflicted*, Hallie. There's nothing ambiguous about it. I *hate* it.'

'But you want Enrico to have whatever it is he needs. And that's admirable.'

The whole point of this exercise was to bring Enrico joy and peace. He might hate the thought of seeing Massimo, might worry that Massimo would let Enrico down again, but the least he could do was hide his anger and concern from his grandfather.

His phone buzzed with an incoming text. He

read the message and nodded. If he wanted to make good on his being-a-better-man resolution…

He stood. 'Are you free for the rest of the day?'

She eyed him warily. He didn't blame her. 'I can be. Why?'

Rather than taunting her with the fruits of his wealth in mean revenge fantasy fashion, he'd lavish her with them instead. 'My meddling matchmaking grandfather asked me earlier if I'd organised those tickets to the opera yet.' He lifted his phone. 'My reservation has just been confirmed for Saturday night in a month's time.'

Her lips twitched the tiniest fraction. 'I'll keep that Saturday night free, then, shall I?'

Should he have asked her properly? But it wasn't a real date, and to pretend otherwise would be disingenuous. 'Hallie, if you'd rather not go or if you've other plans—'

'No other plans.' After lifting her hands, she then let them drop. 'What other plans would I have?'

He lowered himself back to the chair. 'You feel trapped here?'

'Absolutely not. But I'm here to paint a portrait and do whatever is necessary for our charade. Making other plans, beyond ducking out for a walk or to do a little shopping…' She shook her head. 'I'm being paid handsomely to be at your—and Enrico's—beck and call.'

Why did she have to keep mentioning the material benefits of their arrangement? It was almost as if she needed to continually bolster the barriers between them. He thought back to that dance and how quickly their attraction had threatened to consume them, and realised the wisdom of her strategy.

But he could be distant without being bitter and unkind. 'Okay, how's this? If there's anything you want to do while you're here let me know and we'll fit it into our dating schedule.'

She stared at him. 'Okay. Um, thank you.'

He waved her thanks away. 'So opening night at the opera is okay with you?'

She smiled then. 'It's more than okay. I've never been to the opera and…'

She mimed pinching herself, which made him smile, too. 'The opera, however, is a formal affair.' He stood again. 'So let's go buy you a dress.'

She slid off the bench with a frown. 'I can buy my own clothes, Lucas.'

'Ah, but it's part of our deal that I cover all of your expenses.'

'But—'

'And it is a lover-like thing to do.'

'But—'

'And it will make Enrico happy.'

She folded her arms and glared, though there wasn't much heat in it. 'That's not fighting fair.'

He was also hoping that buying her something lovely would ease his guilt at how badly he'd been behaving. He shrugged. 'We need to be seen going on dates. Today we'll go shopping as a sort of date. We'll do the opera in a month's time.'

'And between now and then?'

'We'll work it out.'

An hour later, Lucas ushered Hallie into one of Venice's most exclusive boutiques. She glanced around, her eyes widening at the gowns displayed on various mannequins around the store.

'Oh, my,' she breathed, glancing at him uncertainly before moving across to a mannequin displaying an exquisite lace cocktail dress in dusky pink. She circled it, her eyes wide and her mouth a small soft O. 'Lucas,' she whispered, 'I can't see a price tag.'

He bit back a smile. 'This isn't the kind of establishment that displays price tags.'

The manageress chose that moment to swoop down on them, and when she learned what they were after, three assistants were immediately dispatched to gather an array of gowns while a fourth emerged with champagne on ice. Hallie peeked out from behind the voluminous velvet curtain of the changing room and gave a silent scream, raising her flute towards him in a toast. Chuckling, he raised his glass in return.

She modelled each of the dresses and he weighed in with his opinion, though as far as he was concerned she looked amazing in all of them. It was the dazzled expression in her eyes, though, and her irrepressible smiles that tugged at something deep inside him.

'This is the one,' the manager announced from behind the curtain.

Before he could call out and ask what Hallie thought of it, the curtain was swished open and she stood there in a fitted velvet dress in a shade of green a little deeper than the opal of her eyes, and everything inside him stilled. His mouth went dry.

Hallie glanced at him uncertainly, moistened her lips. 'Maybe it's a little too…much.'

He rose. 'Or maybe it's perfect.'

The sweetheart neckline hugged her curves, exposing the creamy skin of her décolletage and hinting at the intriguing shadow between her breasts. The dress accentuated her small waist and gently flared hips. His blood started to pump too hard, just as it had when they were dancing.

'We'll take it,' he rasped out. He had no idea how he'd cope sitting beside her all evening at the opera when she looked like that, but it'd be a crime for her not to have that dress. Her gaze flew to his and he shook his head. 'You look divine.'

She was whisked back behind the curtain while

the manageress led him to a desk to process the payment. 'Now, is there anything else you would like?'

On impulse he pointed to the dusky pink cocktail dress.

'You have an excellent eye, *signor*. We will make some minor alterations to both dresses and they'll be delivered no later than Friday afternoon.'

A short time later, Hallie sipped a cappuccino and demolished a *torta cioccolato*, and he wondered why he'd refused a sweet. The cake looked delicious.

'I swear, Lucas, I nearly fainted when I was handed the glass of champagne. Do you get the same special treatment when you buy a new suit?'

'Ah, it's all scotch and cigars then.'

She eyed him uncertainly before huffing out a laugh. 'You're pulling my leg. That, however, was an insane amount of fun.'

He sipped his espresso. 'Better than Camden markets?'

'I haven't been to Camden markets for a long time, but I bet they're still fun, too.' She glanced up, noticed the way he eyed her dessert, and spooned up a generous portion and held it out to him. Without thinking, he leaned across, his mouth closing around cake and cream. It was every bit as delicious as it looked.

The spoon wobbled in Hallie's hand. Her eyes had gone dark and wide and they'd fixed on his mouth. A dark swirl of temptation wound around his ankles, making its way up his thighs and groin, and reaching deep inside his chest.

Bad idea.

They eased back at the same moment. She set the spoon to the plate and pushed it away. He tried to stop his heart from pounding out of his chest.

She blotted her lips on her linen napkin, not meeting his eyes. 'That kind of red-carpet treatment could become addictive. I think your wealth must make it hard for you to trust people—women—now. That seems a shame.'

Back when he'd been dreaming his dreams of wealth and success, he hadn't thought there'd be any downsides—like working out whom he could trust—and he hadn't realised then what it would cost him or the sacrifices he'd be forced to make. Would he make the same choices given that time again?

He shook himself. It was pointless asking himself such questions. What he needed to do was focus on the present…and the fact that this woman would never be a part of his future. He pushed away from the table. 'Ready to go?'

She gulped the rest her cappuccino and rose. 'Absolutely.'

A part of him wanted to mourn at the blinkers

that crashed down over her eyes, but he refused to let it. He'd be an idiot to let himself feel anything more for this woman than mild gratitude at the help she was giving him. Aloofness without bitterness or unkindness—that was as much as was required of him. To give anything more would be foolish beyond measure.

Do you seriously think I would ever risk becoming pregnant by you again?

Foolish beyond measure, he repeated to himself.

They had a portrait sitting the following morning. Fran's rigid disapproval and Juliet's teenage death glares, both directed at Hallie whenever they thought he wasn't looking, chafed at Lucas. Rosa, in an ill-thought-out attempt to compensate, babbled incessantly. His temples started to throb. To Hallie's credit, she appeared completely unfazed by any of it as if she hadn't noticed.

Except he knew it would be pricking and cutting at her.

'Enrico,' she said, when Rosa broke off for a moment to draw breath, 'do you remember sneaking out with me one morning on my last visit here to take me on a gondola ride?'

The older man laughed. 'You were trying to be sophisticated and kept saying that water taxis were good enough for you, that gondolas were for the tourists. But *cara*, the look on your face...'

'We watched the sunrise. It was magical.'

He stared from one to the other. Where had he been? Why hadn't he been invited?

A bitter taste coated his tongue. He'd probably been working. Had he been too busy to take Hallie for a gondola ride?

'It has me thinking that's not the only secret, fun-finding mission you've ever embarked on, is it?'

Enrico and Juliet shared a guilty glance. Rosa, the ever-vigilant mother, broke her pose to round on them. 'Okay, out with it. What have the pair of you been up to?'

'There was no harm in it,' Enrico said.

Juliet twisted her hands together. 'Nonno took me to the Taylor Swift concert.'

'Papà, she was supposed to be studying! She—'

'She studies hard enough. She deserved a treat.'

'We had the best time, Mamma.' Juliet pressed her hands to her chest. 'We danced all night.'

Rosa's mouth worked. She glared at her father. 'You *danced*?'

'It's no different to the time he took you to see Le Moulin Rouge when they toured Venice,' Fran pointed out. 'He told Mamma he was taking you to a lecture at the Gallerie dell Accademia.'

Rosa's jaw dropped, and then she barked out a laugh. 'You big tattletale!'

Fran grinned. 'Or the time he sneaked me into his gentlemen's club so I could see what really happened behind those big, dark doors.'

Rosa clapped both hands over her mouth.

And then everyone was laughing and comparing adventures, and Lucas couldn't believe how it had happened. How it had gone from being so awkward to suddenly feeling like a party, like a celebration.

He glanced at Hallie.

As if aware of his gaze, she glanced up and winked. Seizing her sketchpad and a pencil, she set about sketching his family, trying to capture something of their essence—of their joy and connection.

He stared at his family's animated faces, and a balloon of gratitude blossomed in his chest. Hallie had done this. She'd helped his grieving family find laughter and joy. He stared at her, but she resolutely ignored him.

And he knew that was wise and he knew he ought to be grateful for it as well.

CHAPTER SEVEN

'So, Hallie…? I've a favour to ask of you.'

The velvet rasp of Lucas's voice hauled Hallie's attention from her attempts to capture Enrico's impishness and merge it with the wily steeliness that lay beneath. When she glanced up, she found everyone had returned to their places, their faces somehow lighter after the shared laughter.

Lucas raised an eyebrow, an odd warmth in his eyes, and she had to swallow. 'A favour?'

'Yes.'

Every head in the room swung to him—wearing varying expressions of hope, wariness and dismay.

'You used to swim. When I met you in London you were a member of an indoor pool. You swam laps to keep fit.'

'A carry-over of growing up on the east coast of Australia,' she explained with a shrug when everyone turned back to her. 'The beach and swimming are a part of life there. And I'm thinking, given the fact that Venice is surrounded by water, that learning to swim is a big thing here, too.'

Even Juliet nodded.

'In Australia, learning to swim is part of the school curriculum. A lot of us get our lifesaving badges. And as a teenager, summers were synonymous with the beach.'

Everyone stared as if trying to imagine the exotic, sun-filled world she'd grown up in.

'Now, don't get me wrong—' she gestured for everyone to resume their poses and they did so without a murmur of protest '—I love London. It's one of my favourite places on the planet. But London and swimming?' She shook her head.

'I arrived to take up my art residency in the middle of December.' That residency had been the reason she'd been in London when she and Lucas had met. 'I'd never been to Europe before. It had been a balmy thirty-three degrees Celsius when I left home. The two degrees that greeted me when I arrived in London chilled these Australian bones all the way through. I'd never been so cold.'

Enrico and Rosa winced. Fran looked as if she wanted to. Even Juliet's death glare lost some of its zeal.

'Truth be told it was a bit of a culture shock. I was super excited to be in London, but a little homesick, too. When I stumbled across an indoor pool in my neighbourhood... Well, it was a no-brainer. I invested some of my meagre savings to join, which turned out to be a good decision. It kept me grounded. And I made some good friends there.'

'Is that where you met Lucas?' Juliet asked, and then looked as if she'd like to recall her question.

Hallie focused on sketching, though her hand shook a fraction. 'No, but—' she glanced up briefly and smiled '—it was on an evening out with that set of friends when I first met Lucas. So you're nearly right.'

Did he remember? She glanced across; his eyes had darkened and for a brief moment something throbbed between them. Her stupid heart pitter-pattered stupidly.

He cleared his throat. 'I was with work colleagues at a pub for a trivia night—this was back when I was working for the stock exchange—and in walked Hallie with her big smile and unseasonable tan. I couldn't take my eyes off her.'

Mutual. Utterly mutual.

She made herself grin, reminding herself about the game they were playing. 'Lucas might've spent more time in England than Italy at that point, but I can assure you he was Italian through and through from the very first moment I met him—intense, focused and *very* charming.'

As she'd known it would, it made the adults

laugh. Juliet, though, slammed her hands to her hips. 'Then why did you break his heart?'

'Her heart was broken, too,' Lucas inserted, saving Hallie from having to answer.

Her chest ached, as if all that had happened between her and Lucas had left a deep and permanent wound on her heart. One that would never heal.

No! She refused to believe that. She'd carry the scars of her miscarriage and their ill-fated love affair for ever, but she deserved closure and a new start. And she'd fight tooth and nail for it.

'Life can sometimes be complicated, Juliet. Lucas and I wanted different things.'

For instance, she'd been delighted to discover she was pregnant. Lucas hadn't been. For her, the miscarriage had been a tragedy. For him, it had solved a problem.

She pushed those thoughts away. 'It was a hard truth to accept, but I did what I thought was right at the time.' And nothing she'd learned in the years since had proved her wrong. The list she was keeping now proved how right she'd been. 'I never wanted to hurt your cousin, though.'

The younger girl's eyes flashed. 'Are you going to get back together?'

'*Juliet!*'

Rosa looked mortified, but Hallie made herself laugh. 'Oh, Juliet, it was all such a long time ago.' Fingers crossed that sounded suitably ambiguous.

Enrico thrust out his jaw. 'Seven years is nothing!'

Her heart ached then for an entirely different reason. Time must be so precious to him now. He glared and snapped his fingers. 'Seven years is a mere blink. All of you—' he rounded on his family '—should be living your best lives. You should be following your passions and dreams and not letting fear hold you back.'

'Should we not also be trying to live good lives?' Lucas said in the silence following Enrico's proclamation. 'Being kind and showing compassion to our fellow man, having empathy for others and not being selfish?'

All the things his father hadn't been.

'*Sì*, absolutely. We do not stamp all over other people to achieve our dreams. That is a given.'

Something in Lucas's face shifted. Her attention sharpened.

'Are we disappointing you, Nonno?'

Enrico spun to face him. 'No, my dearest Lucas, no! All of you swell my heart with pride. I could not be happier with you all.'

Much embracing ensued, and some tears. A lump lodged in Hallie's throat. Her own family had never been like this, and for a moment she had a vision of what she could've become a part of if she had remained with Lucas all those years ago.

She shook the vision away. What she had to remember was how much of herself she'd risked losing if she'd stayed. She'd made the right decision back then, but it didn't stop her heart—or her eyes—from burning now.

'Come! Back to our places.' Lucas clapped his hands. 'How is Hallie supposed to paint us if we won't stand still?'

Everyone resumed their places.

'And we've strayed off track. I still need to ask her for my favour. Hallie, do you still swim?'

'Uh-huh. As often as I can.'

'Would you consider filling in for my water polo team for a few weeks? One of the women on my team has broken her wrist and our usual substitute is going on a cruise and isn't available.'

'Water polo?' Her jaw dropped. 'I've never played water polo in my life.'

'What does that matter? You can swim and you're relatively fit, and the rules are easy.'

Her mouth opened and closed. *Relatively* fit?

His eyes took on a devilish hue that reminded her of that long ago trivia night. 'And you proved to me yesterday that you can move.'

She was glad she wasn't drinking anything as she'd have sprayed it all over her sketch.

'C'mon, don't be a spoil sport. I promised the team I'd find us a player.'

She tried and failed to smother a laugh. 'Okay, it has the potential to be fun. Why don't I play one match and see how I go?'

'Excellent. We play tonight.'

'*Tonight?* What equipment do I need? I—'

'Did you bring a swimsuit?'

She nodded. She rarely travelled without it.

'Then the rest we can loan to you.'

'Okay, if I'm playing tonight, you all better start versing me on the rules *right* now.'

The others had been watching with a kind of perplexed fascination. But they joined in now to give her various hints and tips.

She didn't know whether to look forward to the match or dread it. As far as *dating* went, though, it was gloriously low-key. And a team sport in a public facility would help them maintain their sense of distance. If she was honest, the idea was inspired.

As the sitting ended, the housekeeper came through with two boxes bearing the name of the boutique where Lucas had taken her shopping. She set them on a side table. 'For you, Signorina Alexander.'

Rosa's eyes lit up when she saw the labels on the boxes. So did Enrico's. Hallie glanced at Lucas and raised her eyebrow the merest fraction and he gave the tiniest of nods in reply.

'Lucas insisted on providing me with a suitable dress for the opera as I'm afraid I didn't pack anything formal. But there ought to be only one box so I expect there's been some mistake. Would you like to see, though? It's the most beautiful dress I've ever worn.'

'Sì, cara,' Enrico said, gesturing impatiently.

She untied the ribbon on the top box and lifted layers of tissue paper out, her breath catching at the beautiful deep green of the lush material. Carefully lifting it out, she held it against herself and turned. 'It's exquisite, isn't it?'

Mouths dropped open. Even Juliet clasped her hands beneath her chin.

'This will probably sound terribly gauche to you all, but I've never been inside a boutique that doesn't display the prices before. And there was champagne! I felt like Cinderella.'

The smile that spread across Enrico's face lifted something inside her. She was glad she was here; glad she'd agreed to do this thing.

She very carefully placed it back inside its box and frowned at the other. This one had to be a mistake. 'It feels wrong to open it.'

'Open the box, Hallie.'

That was Lucas. She glanced at him uncertainly. Maybe he'd ordered some accompanying lingerie to go with the dress. In which case she'd better gird her loins.

'Come, come, *cara*, do as Lucas says,' Enrico ordered as they all huddled around her.

With a little thrill, she lifted the lid and sifted through the tissue paper until the dress was revealed. 'Oh!' The breath left her lungs on a whoosh.

Very slowly, she lifted it out and everyone gasped and oohed. Rosa reached out tentative fingers to touch the dusky pink lace. 'Oh, Hallie…'

She glanced at Lucas, a lump in her throat.

'It was on one of the mannequins when we entered the shop and I could tell that Hallie had fallen in love with it.'

They were playing a game, a charade, creating a fake reality. But this was still a ridiculously thoughtful gesture. 'Oh, Lucas, you didn't have to buy it for me.'

'I know, but I wanted to. And the look on your face just now made it worthwhile.'

He smiled in a way he didn't mean—a lover-like way—but it made the heat gather in her veins all the same. Reaching up on tiptoe, she kissed his cheek. 'Thank you. I'll treasure it.' And while she knew she was playing a role, it didn't feel that way. She *would* treasure this dress for ever.

She carefully placed the dress back into its tissue paper nest while Rosa helped her father upstairs for a rest. Juliet, who had Wednesday mornings free from classes but was expected at the auditorium for practice this afternoon, raced off to get ready.

'Hallie.' She glanced around to find Fran standing at her elbow. 'Thank you.'

She straightened. 'No thanks are necessary, Fran. It's an honour and a pleasure to paint your family's portrait.'

'I do not refer to that. I meant for making that conversation happen during the sitting. Our family has been shrouded in grief since Enrico's diagnosis. But that—' she gestured to the now empty chairs '—the sharing of our recollections, of the silly things we've done with Enrico, was a joy. And sorely needed.'

'That was you and your family's doing. Not mine.'

'You initiated the conversation, made the space for it, and encouraged it to happen. You were instrumental, Hallie, and I'm very grateful.'

She swallowed a funny lump. 'Your family deserves all the joy in the world, Fran.'

'I want to apologise for being less than welcoming to you when you first arrived. I—'

'No, don't!' She waved the apology away. 'It's only right that you should be protective of your nephew. I'm glad Lucas has such a family.'

The other woman hesitated. 'If you and Lucas truly did want different things back then, Hallie, then you did the right thing. However hard it was on the both of you at the time. Otherwise, you'd have been torn for ever, and that is no way to live a life.'

The older woman patted Hallie's shoulder and left.

She and Lucas still wanted different things. She couldn't let herself forget that. *That* needed to go on her list.

Dragging in a breath, she turned to him. He sat in a chair on the other side of the room waiting with a patience she found hard to associate with him. Sitting quietly was something he'd never been able to do seven years ago. He'd been too busy working and striving towards the success he'd craved.

What had changed? Could he sit quietly now because he'd achieved all he'd set out to do? She went to ask, but bit the questions back. The two of them were only pretending to be reconciling. They weren't the real deal. She needed to leave the past behind. All and any mention of it had the potential to turn things between them into a battlefield again, and she'd avoid that if she could.

'Everything okay?'

He sauntered across to help her gather up her equipment. She shot him a quick smile. 'Very okay.'

'Fran?'

'Very okay,' she repeated.

He helped her collect up her equipment. 'I'm sorry things became so personal just then,' he said as they climbed the stairs to her studio.

'I'm not. It helped clear the air. Besides, it's paved the way nicely for this burgeoning relationship of ours.'

Fake relationship.

'And Enrico's face when he saw the dresses...' *That* had been worth the price of admission alone.

'He was delighted.'

She grinned. 'Understatement much?'

He laughed. 'It was excellent timing, too. Most serendipitous.'

She feigned shock. 'You mean you didn't deliberately arrange it?'

'Alas, no. Not even I'm that good.'

She wasn't so sure about that.

'Hallie, I want to thank you for sharing the story about Enrico taking you for a gondola ride. It opened a door that...'

He looked so lost for a moment, she couldn't stop from reaching out and placing a hand on his arm. Beneath her fingers, his skin pulsed with a warmth that had her wanting to draw nearer.

He stared at her hand, the pulse in his throat throbbing to life.

She snatched it back and made a mental note to avoid touching him as much as possible in the future. 'Sometimes it's hard to remember the good times when we're in the midst of grief. Sometimes someone not in the immediate circle can find a way in.'

'You did it deliberately?'

She forced her legs up the final steps and along the corridor to her studio. Anyone with eyes in their heads could see the family needed some fun and respite. 'I wanted to find a way to stop everyone from looking so wooden.'

She didn't know why she lied. But it was easier to maintain her own distance when Lucas treated her like a pariah. He didn't say anything, just placed the items he'd carried onto the long cabinet. She busied herself putting things away.

'May I look?'

She turned to find him holding her sketchpad. 'Sure.'

Moving closer, but not too close, she surveyed her work with a critical eye as he turned the pages.

When he reached the end, he stared at her with something like awe. 'These are extraordinary. You've captured the essence of each of us.'

Taking the sketchpad from him, she flicked through the pages again. They weren't *extraordinary*, but... 'I'm pleased with them.' It had been a good session.

'What will you do with these once the portrait is completed?'

'Lucas, these are just preliminary sketches.' It seemed unkind to tell him they'd be destroyed. 'I—'

'May I have them when you're done?'

She huffed out a laugh. 'If you want.'

His eyes lit up as if she'd given him a great prize. If she wasn't careful she'd start believing he meant it—start believing in *him* again—and she couldn't afford to do that.

She'd wanted their baby. He hadn't. *That* was the moment her heart had started to break seven years ago. Work had meant more to him than the family they were creating. Just like her father's work had always meant more to him than she and her mother ever had. She couldn't let herself forget that.

'Did you talk to Enrico about Massimo?' she asked, deliberately changing the subject.

He set the sketches down. 'He's beside himself with delight at my offer to help find him.'

She wrinkled her nose. 'We need to discuss how we're going to do that. How we're going to start the search—'

'Oh, I know where he is.'

Her jaw dropped. She turned to stare.

One broad shoulder lifted. 'It's one of the advantages of being wealthy. I know people who can get things done.'

'Where is he?'

'Here in Venice. The address will mean nothing to you.' But he rattled the address off all the same.

He was right; it meant nothing. 'When…?'

'Not today.'

No, Lucas needed time to strengthen the walls around his heart before facing his father. She understood that. But they couldn't delay indefinitely. 'Soon,' she said.

'Soon,' he echoed.

The moment Hallie emerged from the dressing room with the other women on his water polo team, wearing her one-piece swimsuit, a swimming cap, and with a pair of swimming goggles dangling from her fingers, Lucas's mouth dried and his skin tightened. In principle, this idea had seemed simple. He and Hallie needed to spend time together, and spending that time in the company of others had seemed a safer option than being alone with her. He should've known that in practice it would be a vastly different enterprise.

Not impossible, though. He clenched his jaw. He *would* make this work. He wouldn't be the one to destroy the peace Enrico deserved. He simply needed to view this as a series of inoculations. Hallie was a virus and through this continual contact with her, he was slowly but surely inoculating himself against the effect she had on him.

Except she didn't look like a virus. She looked like every man's dream with her long shapely legs, hips that gently flared, and while no one would ever describe Hallie as busty, her chest was perfection. Things that shouldn't twitched to life. He gave thanks he was in the water where no one would see.

Before he could drag his gaze away and feign interest in something else, her eyes swept across the pool, widening when they landed on him. Her lips parted, her feet faltered and the knuckles on the hand that held the goggles turned white. Wind roared in his ears when she moistened her lips and touched a hand to her throat.

'The pool is heated to twenty-two degrees Celsius,' he snapped.

She blinked, her cheeks turning pink.

'Jump in and let's take you through your paces.'

Hallie was strong in the water and quick. He tried to focus on what she was doing rather than the lines of her body and how she flowed through the water, or the way her chest lifted when she surged up for a high ball. Her upper body strength wasn't as well developed as some of the other members of the team, but she had a good eye.

She shrugged when he said as much. 'That's thanks to years of playing netball.'

He'd watched her play once, early in their relationship, before he and Doug had gone into business together and things had become so hectic. He hadn't been able to take his eyes off her back then.

You're not doing much better now...

He motioned for Simona, their team captain, to take over Hallie's training and joined a couple of the men at the net to pelt the goal with all of his might.

Antonio clapped him on the shoulder. 'You shoot like that tonight and we'll be unstoppable.'

'It's easy when there's no opposition bearing down on me.'

They both laughed and some of his tension dissipated.

The game was fast and furious, and Hallie made mistakes—of course she did—but not as many as he'd have expected. And when all was said and done, they all made mistakes—misread the play, misjudged a pass—but laughter rang around the pool along with much good-natured teasing. Hallie's laughter sounded as often as everyone else's and he was glad of it. She was doing him and his family a favour and he wanted her to have fun—not to find being in Venice a chore.

'What did you think?' he asked as they puttered home. The speed limit on the canals was a sedate seven kilometres per hour to protect the buildings and lagoon against erosion from wave movement. When he'd first come to live here, the enforced leisurely pace had chafed at him.

'I loved it! It was so much fun.'

'Am I correct in assuming you'd be happy to continue playing water polo for the duration of your stay?'

'Yes, please. I *really* want to score a goal next week. Your goal was pretty spectacular.'

Do not puff your chest out. 'Thank you.'

'How long have you been playing?'

Her eyes sparkled and her skin glowed. The exercise had been good for her. 'Four years now, I think.'

She blinked. 'Really?'

He focused on steering the boat. 'You sound surprised?'

'I suppose I am. Back when we were together you didn't have time for things like sport.'

Things inside him clenched. He'd been busy consolidating Cormack and Quinn Holdings, the company he and Doug had set up—fighting the hostile forces that had been intent on taking them over. It had taken his every resource to keep them afloat. It had taken his every spare moment. They'd been a David in a sea of Goliaths.

'Also, you're really good at it.'

Her words snapped him out of his sombre reflections, and she rolled her eyes. 'My observations weren't supposed to make you morose. They weren't a criticism.'

'I know.'

Seven years ago they had been, though. Her refrain back then had been *There's more to life than work*. He'd sworn to her that once the business was established, he'd ease back on his hours. He'd never intended to work those insane hours for ever.

But until Cormack and Quinn was a success, he'd had to work all the hours of the day. He'd been so driven, had so much he'd wanted to prove to the world. And he'd needed to make his mother's sacrifice count. For God's sake, Nicola Quinn had sacrificed her life for him. Proving that her faith hadn't been misplaced had seemed the least he could do.

Nicola was only forty when she'd discovered she had an inoperable brain tumour. A drug not yet on the NHS might've prolonged her life, maybe even have saved it, but she'd refused it. The treatment would've taken all of their life savings—money she'd squirrelled away for Lucas's education. Though he'd known about none of this until after her death.

He'd been nineteen at the time—an adult! He could've taken out student loans. Her life had been worth his education ten times over. He'd never been given the opportunity to plead his case, though, because she'd kept her illness from him until the very end. She'd wanted to spare him the pain and angst of watching her die. And she'd wanted him to remain focused on his studies.

In hindsight, he supposed it had been easy enough to do. He'd gone off to university in London while she'd remained in Lancaster. They'd spoken often on the phone and he'd made the occasional weekend trek home. His mother, though, had been a lifelong migraine sufferer, so it hadn't seemed unusual to him when she'd excuse herself to lie down for a couple of hours or had an early night when he did visit.

He'd turned it over in his mind a million times—he should've realised something was wrong. Even now, the horror that he hadn't, the crippling guilt, could wake him in the middle of the night lathered in sweat.

His mother had continually told him that a good education was his ticket to a better life. He'd needed to make her sacrifice count, to make her dreams for him a reality. Not to do so would've been a betrayal of everything she'd stood for. He'd have never been able to live with himself.

And he'd been determined to leave poverty behind him for ever—to never again lose someone he loved because they couldn't afford medical treatment.

Hallie had never understood that, and he'd

resented the pressure she'd put on him to take time out from work *to smell the roses*. The roses could darn well wait. Though, in the end, Hallie had refused to.

Dragging in a breath, he told himself that was all in the past and to let it go. Hallie had had her own demons he'd never fully understood—a morbid fear of suffering the same fate as her mother. They'd been young. Her lack of faith in him had wounded him deeply, but he could see now how her own fears coupled with her grief over the miscarriage might've spiralled out of control.

His mother had taught him to protect the people he loved by hiding his pain from them, by shielding them from it. He'd wanted to protect Hallie as much as he could, to be strong for her, to shield her just as Nicola had done for him.

His chest clenched. He'd wanted to be strong and stoical for Hallie in the way he'd never had the chance to be strong and stoical for his mother. But if he'd shared his grief with her, would she have turned towards him rather than away from him? Rather than driving a wedge between them, could their shared grief have drawn them closer?

Had his mother been wrong?

He shied away from that thought. It was too late, all too late. What was the point in obsessing over it now?

Except he'd started to see how much his own stoicism had been a factor in all that had gone wrong between him and Hallie. He'd hidden his vulnerability and his pain, and in doing so she'd misinterpreted it. He could see now how it had probably made her feel shut out and alone. To admit as much out loud might lighten his load, but in all likelihood, it would only add to hers. He had no right to do that. She'd told him in Sydney that she didn't want to talk about it.

He glanced across, and the wide-eyed way she took in the sights chased his more sombre thoughts away. 'How much of Venice have you seen so far on this visit?' A bad taste stretched through his mouth. He ought to know the answer to this, but... 'How much did you see seven years ago?'

'A bit.'

He read between the lines. She hadn't seen much at all. That was a travesty.

'There's so much art here, Hallie.' Art that she would love. 'We need to date, but those dates don't have to be onerous. We can do things you'll enjoy.' Like sightseeing and visiting art galleries. 'Why don't we become tourists?' He could show her the city that had come to mean so much to him.

Her smile—broad and full of delight—was his reward. 'I'd love that!'

CHAPTER EIGHT

'WHAT I REMEMBER most about Lucas coming into our lives was how efficiently he slid into a consulting role at La Amatissima and turned our fortunes around,' Fran said, referring to the Zaneri family's high-end cosmetic company. The company was over a hundred years old and the brand one of the most prestigious in Italy.

Hallie's paintbrush stilled. The sittings, or at least the number of sittings they were currently having, weren't strictly necessary. But everyone looked forward to them so much she hadn't had the heart to curtail them.

Lucas probably realised. If he remembered half as much from their time together as she did, he'd recall how long she'd needed clients or models to sit for a portrait. But then she recalled how obsessed he'd been with work and figured maybe not.

When the family gathered for these sittings, it had become commonplace for Hallie to ask a question that would prompt a flood of nostalgic anecdotes. Warmth and laughter would ensue, cementing the family's closeness.

'I've worked in business all of my adult life,' Fran continued. 'I'm good at what I do.' She spoke the truth. As the head of La Amatissima, she had a reputation for being tough and level-headed— an expert in her field. 'But seeing Lucas in action left me speechless.'

'*Sì.*' Enrico nodded. 'If it had not been for Lucas, La Amatissima would have gone into receivership.'

Hallie's jaw dropped.

'Lucas cut through the layers of tradition that had made of us prisoners, and *presto*—' Enrico snapped his fingers '—there was light again at the end of the tunnel.'

'And he refused money, thanks, kudos…*anything.*'

'We're family.' Lucas rolled his shoulders. 'We help each other.'

'You *saved* La Amatissima?' Hallie blurted out.

Every eye in the room turned to her and then to Lucas.

'Oh, Lucas,' Rosa murmured. 'You never told Hallie?'

The stricken expression on Enrico's, Fran's and Rosa's faces pierced Hallie's heart. It was as if they suddenly held themselves responsible for Lucas and Hallie's breakup seven years ago.

Lucas's dark eyes throbbed into hers and she shook herself. 'Oh, no, Rosa, I knew he was helping out.'

Shoulders and jaws started to relax again.

'I just hadn't realised what a significant role he'd played. He's far too humble.' She made her voice light, though inside she felt as heavy as lead. Why hadn't he told her? 'No wonder you're all so proud of him.'

She moved the conversation into other channels, but the knowledge that she'd known none of this chafed at her.

Twenty minutes later, she called a halt to the session. As usual, Lucas helped carry her things back up to the studio. She glanced across as he set her palette, brushes and sketchpad onto the bench. He seemed lost in his thoughts.

'Can I ask you something?'

He turned. 'Shoot.'

'Why didn't you tell me La Amatissima was in so much trouble? Or that you helped save it?'

He rubbed a hand over his face before gesturing to the fridge. 'Would you like a snack?'

'No.' She wrestled with herself for a moment before adding, 'Thank you.'

After striding across to the French windows, she swung them open and stepped outside to draw air not scented with the spice of Lucas's cologne into her lungs.

Traffic chugged along the canal below—water

taxis, speedboats and beautifully elegant gondolas. If she angled herself just so, she could see the Grand Canal farther along with its even busier procession of traffic.

He stepped out behind her. 'You're angry?'

She wasn't sure what she was. Confused? Sad? Tired? 'I just don't know why you'd keep something that big from me.'

He lowered his tall frame to one of the chairs and rested his elbows on his knees, his fingers steepling beneath his chin. 'If we're being honest, I suppose my reasons were both good and bad,' he finally said. 'You were already worried about how much I was working, and telling you how much more I'd taken on would've led to another fight. I didn't want that.'

Letting out a breath, she dropped to the seat beside him. 'What were your other reasons?'

'You'd recently told me you were pregnant and I didn't want you worrying. It was more important that you and the baby were well and healthy.'

She blinked.

He thrust out his jaw. 'And maybe that's paternalistic.'

Or maybe it was just plain protective. He might not have welcomed her pregnancy, but she'd never doubted that he'd wanted her to be well and healthy. He was silent for a long moment. 'After the miscarriage, I didn't want to add to your grief.'

She'd felt totally alone.

And alone in her grief, too. She'd wanted the baby with her whole heart, but it had never been anything more than a burden to him. And for a short period of time, she'd wanted to disappear. Just like her mother had done. That was when she'd known she had to leave.

'Would it have made any difference if you'd known I was trying to save La Amatissima? Would you have stayed?'

She shook herself, tried to stop apathy and re-membered grief from claiming her. 'I honestly don't know, Lucas. Maybe it would've helped to know that there was so much at stake and so much responsibility resting on your shoulders. But maybe it would've overwhelmed me even more.'

He eased back, stretched his long legs out to the side so as to not crowd her, but rather than looking relaxed his whole body seemed to sag. 'I thought you understood the time commit-ment that setting up Cormack and Quinn would demand of me. Doug and I had put all of our money into it. I couldn't just pick it up and set it down at will—I needed to give it everything. And then the thought of seeing Enrico and the others lose their family company, too, was un-thinkable to me. I felt honour bound to help.'

She'd not figured in his calculations at all.

'I took you for granted. I can see that now.'

She glanced at him, surprised.

'It's just… I thought you'd be there, would stick beside me, through everything.'

'I did, too. I just hadn't realised…'

'What?'

'That it would be so one-sided—me there for you, but you—' she shrugged '—nowhere to be seen.'

'I'd have repaid your patience tenfold. Once we'd got through that initial struggle, I'd have been there for you whenever you needed me.'

'I needed you *then*, Lucas, not at some indeterminate time in the future.'

They both turned back to stare out at the canal, both breathing hard.

She struggled to keep her voice neutral. 'I understood why you never wanted to live in poverty again, and that you were building a life that ensured you'd never have to face those same deprivations. But I never understood why you couldn't be happy with being *simply* successful. You were obsessed with being *stratospherically* successful. We'd have been fine on a fraction of the money you were making and—'

'*Fine* wasn't good enough!' His hands clenched. 'Damn it, Hallie, I was never again letting someone I loved die—you, the new family I'd found,

Doug, *anyone*—because they couldn't afford medical treatment that would save their lives.'

She froze. The way his mother had died? Deep inside, her heart broke a little more, though this time for him. *Oh, Lucas.*

'My mother chose my education over her own life, Hallie. I couldn't let her down. I had to succeed. I *had* to make her proud.'

They were both silent after that, doggedly staring at the canal. He pulled in a breath. 'None of that changes the fact that I should've told you how embroiled I was in saving La Amatissima. I'm sorry.'

She stared at her hands and willed the old bitterness away. 'It doesn't matter any more. It's in the past. Ancient history.' Even if they could redo it, there was no guarantee the outcome would've been any happier.

Because she couldn't forget that she'd loved the baby she was carrying, while he hadn't. And fair or unfair, she didn't think she'd ever be able to forgive him for that.

'I can't believe you haven't visited St Mark's Square yet this visit.'

Hallie shrugged at Lucas's incredulous expression. 'When I've not been painting, I've been exploring the area around the palazzo.' There were shops, museums, parks and galleries enough to keep her busy in that quarter. 'It's been fun to explore a part of the city a lot of tourists don't get an opportunity to experience.'

'And busy swimming laps at the swim centre, too, I hear.'

She'd started swimming laps at the aquatic centre where they played water polo, trying to tame the strange restlessness that had taken hold of her, but… How did he know about that?

He shrugged at the question in her eyes. 'You've been seen. And Venice is small.'

Not that small. Was he keeping tabs on her, making sure she didn't do anything that would threaten the illusion of their developing romance? Given the financial investment he'd already made, she supposed she couldn't blame him.

It was the weekend and they were supposedly on a date. The two of them were doing their utmost to be on their best and most polite behaviour.

'Well, the thing is,' she said, leaning in closer as if imparting a secret, 'I've started playing for this amazing water polo team. I'm in training so I don't lose my spot.'

He laughed. A genuine laugh rather than the polite smiles she'd had to endure so far. She found herself smiling, too.

'The thing is, as I've told you, I *really* want to score a goal.'

He huffed out another laugh, before gesturing

around. 'Swim your laps if you must, but you have to see inside the basilica again.'

She'd seen it on her first visit all those years ago and had been blown away. She was eager to see it again.

'And the Doge's Palace is a must.'

They spent a couple of happy hours playing tourist, Hallie alternately gasping and exclaiming, and then silently staring in awe at the art. And every time she did, Lucas's shoulders went back a little more, as if proud of being able to show her something so amazing.

She gazed, stunned all over again, at the Pala d'Oro—the basilica's ornate high altar—and surveyed the stunning mosaics and the sparkling treasury with her mouth agape. She tried to imagine the conversations the various artists of the time must've had.

In the Doge's Palace she stared at the paintings in the Chamber of the Great Council and the Square Atrium until her eyes ached. She even forgot herself at one point and lectured Lucas on the importance of Tintoretto's *Paradise*, although he was probably aware of it already.

She wrinkled her nose. 'Sorry, I get carried away. It's amazing to see these things.'

'Don't apologise. It's nice to see you so…'

Their gazes caught and clung, something arced between them—something she desperately tried to resist. Nice to see her so *what*?

'Animated,' he finished, dragging his gaze away. 'You always could lose yourself in a painting or a fine sculpture. It's—' He broke off as if disconcerted by what he'd been about to say.

'It's what?'

'I'm just glad there's something you can enjoy while you're here. After browbeating you into coming to Venice—'

'You didn't *browbeat* me!'

'Using Enrico's illness as leverage was emotionally manipulative.'

'Ah, but that's down to Enrico not you. I always had the option of refusing the commission. I didn't feel manipulated, Lucas. I'm being paid generously for my time—at the end of all this I'll own a prime piece of real estate.' She hauled in a breath, her heart starting to thump. 'And...'

His gaze sharpened. 'And?'

She pressed her hands together. Was she going to do this?

She was. She really was. 'It's time to launch myself on the European art scene. I've been playing it safe in my own little world for too long. But this commission has given me the perfect entrée into launching myself here. So don't forget that I'm benefitting from the arrangement, too.'

He leaned towards her. 'That's great news, Hallie. You'll take Europe by storm, be the biggest sensation.' He smiled one of those smiles that lit his eyes with mischief and made him look so like Enrico. 'My grandfather will take credit for this, you know.'

She gurgled out a laugh.

He clapped his hands. 'This calls for celebration. Gelato?'

'Yes, please!'

A short while later they sat on a bench overlooking the Grand Canal eating gelato. It felt like they ought to be in a movie.

The silence was companionable and easy, and Lucas couldn't explain why, but it worried him. He couldn't let this feeling of peace and their old easy familiarity lull him into a false sense of security. He watched her lick her boysenberry swirl gelato and his stomach—not to mention other things—clenched.

Don't watch her eat the gelato.

Dragging his gaze away, he focused on his own coffee bean crunch. He and Hallie had made mistakes in the past—mistakes he had no intention of repeating. Despite the show they were putting on for his family, they didn't have a future together.

For God's sake, she thought him a heartless monster who hadn't mourned their unborn child.

Tell her the truth, then.

And why would she believe him? The fact was he hadn't jumped for joy when she'd first told him about the pregnancy. He'd known his reaction had disappointed her, but it didn't mean he hadn't cared. Had she really thought it unreasonable of him to be worried, concerned, uneasy? He'd felt overwhelmed; the weight pressing down on him had been crippling. He'd been worried that he'd let everyone down.

The guilt had ravaged him afterwards. He'd felt that he'd deserved to be punished for not being more joyful, more grateful. Though Hallie hadn't deserved any such thing. She'd loved their baby from the very first. Maybe the stoicism he'd armoured himself with had been an attempt to keep that guilt at bay? At the time, though, he'd told himself that it wasn't her job to make him feel better. It had been his job to be there for her.

Except his silence had had the opposite effect.

And now there was too much hurt and resentment, too much water under the bridge. There was no purpose in blurting any of it out now. He wasn't risking his heart again, and nor was she. They were both adamant about that. Which should've made this easier. Except *nothing* about this was easy.

He was sorry she'd suffered so much. He wished her heart hadn't been as badly broken as his. But… *I've lost faith in this.* Meaning she'd lost faith in him. She'd thrown those words at him, stark and uncompromising, shattering his world into a million pieces. Just like that.

He'd never give her the power to do that again. He'd believed in her. Utterly. But she hadn't believed in him.

It doesn't mean you can't be friendly.

Except *friendly* wasn't the way he felt about her. Unfortunately. Which is why he needed to keep his gaze averted while she ate her gelato. Keeping his eyes trained on a *vaporetto*—a water taxi—he welcomed the metallic rattling of its ramp clattering into place and the chattering of the passenger who spilled from its depths.

'Right!' Hallie slapped a hand to her knee. 'What stories are we going to tell everyone about our date when we get back to the palazzo? Because everyone is going to be curious. Questions will be asked.' She pointed her waffle cone in his direction before taking a bite.

Don't watch her eat the gelato. Don't get caught up on the shape of her lips, or what they might taste like, or how they would feel against your body or...anything!

His heart beat too hard. He did what he could to pull himself back into straight lines.

'And your family won't be put off with a tepid noncommittal *good.*'

At the comical expression on her face, he found himself laughing unexpectedly, his shoulders unclenching a fraction. Knowing Hallie, she'd sensed his tension, and was trying to ease it in an effort to keep things easy and relaxed between them. It was the kind of thing she'd do. Because she *wasn't* the monster he'd created in his mind. The monster he'd created in an effort to make himself feel better, to convince himself that he was better off without her.

They'd wanted different things; that was what she'd told Fran. Why couldn't he have come up with an explanation as simple and blameless?

'Lucas?'

He shook himself. He needed to do his part at keeping things easy between them, too. 'I think you'll wax lyrical about all of the art you've seen—you won't be able to contain yourself—while I smile enigmatically.'

'So I have to do all the heavy lifting?' she said in mock outrage.

'I'll have you know enigmatic smiles are harder than you think.' It was his turn to point his waffle cone at her. 'And don't forget you're getting a prime piece of real estate as a reward.'

'And the opportunity to launch myself on Europe. Don't forget that, or—'

She broke off to gesture to the Grand Canal and mimed pinching herself. He shook his head and made himself laugh, but...

Please, God, let her finish her gelato soon.

'You should slip my European move into the conversation, at some point.'

'Good idea.' It'd add veracity to the growing seriousness of their relationship. *Alleged relationship.* 'I can already see the way Enrico's face will light up.'

She finished her gelato, wiped her fingers on a paper serviette and he sagged. He felt as if he'd survived an ordeal.

'And later in the week,' she added, 'if we happen to be watching TV with Enrico, Rosa and Juliet, we should bicker about what to watch on the weekend. I'll have my heart set on a period drama, but as we all know—' luscious lips twitched '—period dramas are not your favourite.' She stuck her nose in the air. 'Of course you'll give in.'

She said it to make him laugh, but he couldn't. Coffee bean crunch churned in his stomach. 'You remember everything.'

She stilled at whatever she saw in his face.

She remembered it all with the same level of detail that he did. He didn't know why that should shake him up so much. Did she still wake up in the middle of the night yearning for what they'd once had?

He studied her face—he'd once known its every line. It had lost its youthful plumpness, sculpted now into something stronger and finer, but he'd bet his entire fortune that if they kissed, the fire between them would burn just as fiercely. If—

He shot to his feet. He had to stop thinking like this. It might've been unfair of him to blame Hallie so comprehensively for their breakup, but it didn't change the fact that they didn't have a future. She'd wanted something different back then and he'd never been able to provide it. He glanced back at her. She stared out at the passing boats, but a pulse pounded at the base of her throat and she shredded the serviette with shaking fingers.

'We should go.' He was careful to keep his voice low.

'You should sit.' She didn't look at him as she spoke. She gathered up the shredded bits of serviette and dropped them into a nearby bin. 'We need to talk about a less fun topic now. Massimo.'

His father's name was an icy dash that chased the heat from his veins. He collapsed back down beside her. Though he was careful to keep a safe distance between them.

'I don't want to rush you, Lucas.'

She sighed and he almost turned to look at her. *Not wise.*

'But it's been nearly a fortnight since Enrico asked me to contact him, and he asked me yesterday how things were progressing.'

'What did you say?'

'That enquiries were underway and I expected to have news soon.'

'Thank you for keeping things general.' If Enrico knew that Lucas already had Massimo's address…

'I understand your reluctance to see Massimo, and I'll totally understand if you want nothing more to do with any of this. If you give me the address, I can take things from here.'

It was a kind offer and he was tempted. Massimo had rejected him before he'd been born, had abandoned Nicola to a life of hardship and penury. He'd be glad to never clap eyes on the man. And yet, it felt wrong to leave it to Hallie. This task should never have fallen to her.

He didn't like the thought of her going to that part of town on her own, either.

Pulling out his phone, he checked his schedule. 'How's Thursday afternoon? Are you free?'

She nodded.

'We'll go and see him then.'

'You're sure?'

He was far from sure but he refused to let her carry out his family's dirty work on her own. 'Yes.'

Thursday came around far too quickly.

Lucas stared at the address on his phone. 'This is the place.'

Hallie gazed upwards. 'The building looks ancient.'

'It used to be a monastery.' His hands clenched

and unclenched. 'The building was decommissioned last century and a charitable organisation now uses it to, among other things, offer shelter to the homeless.' It was the last place he'd expected to find Massimo.

'Your father is homeless?' She folded her arms. 'In which case Enrico's interest in seeing him has occurred at a convenient time.'

The way her lips thinned had warmth stealing through him. She didn't think any better of Massimo than he did. He resented Massimo to the very marrow of his bones. He didn't trust the man. The fact that Hallie, too, was on her guard made him breathe easier.

Blowing out a breath, she leaned forward and rang the bell.

They were shown to a reception room and asked to wait. A short time later an older man Lucas would never have recognised as Massimo if he'd passed him on the street, shuffled into the room. The two men had never met, but he'd seen the family photographs.

Massimo halted when he saw Lucas. 'They told me a *Signorina* Hallie Alexander wished to see me.'

Hallie stood. 'I'm Hallie Alexander, Signor Zaneri.' She glanced between the two men and gestured towards Lucas. 'Do you know who this is?'

'I do. His name is Lucas Quinn, and he is the

son that, to my eternal shame, I refused to recognise as my own.'

'I doubt that gave you too many pangs until
you found yourself in your current straitened cir-
cumstances,' Lucas drawled, remaining seated.

Massimo stared back, his eyes unwavering.
'I deserve your resentment.'

Just as well as he had it in spades. Though
he found it difficult to square this man with the
selfish reckless playboy he'd formerly imagined.

Hallie motioned the older man to a seat. Typ-
ically polite, though she didn't smile. 'We've
come on an errand from your father, Enrico.'

Massimo's gaze sharpened. *'Papà?'*

'He wishes to see you.'

Massimo frowned. 'This is…unexpected.' He
turned to Lucas. 'I think you would prefer me
to stay away, *si*?'

He didn't deny it, but… 'It's not about what I
want. It's about what Enrico wants. He's dying,
and for some reason wishes to see you before
he quits this earth.'

Massimo, who'd lowered himself to a chair,
shot to his feet again. *'Mio Dio!'* His face turned
grey.

Hallie shot Lucas a glare that he suspected
he deserved. Massimo might be a miserable excuse for a father, but this was his own father
they were talking about. Enrico was the best of

men. He had to have left a mark, even on someone like Massimo.

'I'm sorry if that comes as a shock to you,' he forced from stiff lips. The burn in his heart eased a fraction at the smile Hallie sent him.

'I do not deserve consideration from you.' Massimo spoke woodenly. 'Please do not apologise to me.'

Lucas blinked.

Hallie leapt in. 'Signor Zaneri. If we arrange it, will you come and see him?'

'If he wishes to see me, *sì*. I will deny him nothing.'

'Thank you.'

He wanted to roll his eyes at her impeccable manners, but at the same time he was grateful for them.

'Is there a number we can contact you on?'

'I do not have a phone, but I can give you the office number here.'

Hallie jotted down the number he rattled off and then rose. 'Thank you for seeing us. We'll be in touch.'

Without another word, Lucas rose and moved with her to the door.

'Lucas?'

He froze at the sound of his name on the other man's lips.

'I apologise for never acknowledging you. For never being there for you or being a father to you.'

He swung around. 'You think an apology will change anything?'

'It changes nothing, this I know. But nor is there any denying that you deserve an apology from me.' He stared at his hands before lifting his head to meet Lucas's glare. 'I sit in on the twelve-step programmes here and have learned the importance of apologising to the people one has injured.'

'And with one apology you think you can allay the guilt of sentencing my mother and me to a life of poverty?'

'The guilt will never be allayed!' Fire flashed from the older man's eyes. 'But if it is any consolation, I am reaping what I have sown. All of my recklessness and selfishness, my greed, has led me to this place.' He gestured around. 'Where I have nothing and no one.' He lifted his chin. 'This is what I deserve and I will submit to it with grace, but I cannot deny that my regrets are bitter and many.'

Lucas's heart pounded. It *should* be a consolation. Massimo had brought this on himself. But no matter how hard he tried to summon it, satisfaction refused to fill him.

'And while you will not believe me, I have no plans to take advantage of Enrico's generosity. I will not take money from him.'

Lucas snorted his disbelief.

'I will not further my own interests or my own

comfort at Enrico's expense. I have done nothing in my life to earn it, but before I die I would like to gain a grain of your respect.'

Lucas couldn't speak. Hallie slipped a hand into the crook of his arm and with a soft, *'Arrivederci...'* led him away.

When the door of the building closed behind them and they stood on the street once more, she let out a long breath. 'Could that have been any more uncomfortable?' She patted his arm and then released him and straightened her blouse. 'Yet, we survived it.'

He wanted to hug her for being in this with him.

'And mission accomplished!' She dusted off her hands. 'He agreed to see Enrico.'

She sent him a small smile then. Taking her hand, he squeezed it. 'Thank you, Hallie. Thank you for…everything.'

She squeezed his hand back. 'You're welcome.' And then she rolled her eyes, nudged his shoulder with hers. 'But, God, Lucas, you now need to buy me a wine, *pronto.*'

He couldn't help it. He laughed. And then he leaned forward and pressed his lips to hers.

CHAPTER NINE

THE KISS TOOK Hallie completely off guard. There'd been no heated glances to raise alarm bells, no flashes of desire or lust, no frozen moments of burning, longing need.

Warmth—yes.

Relief—yes.

A sense of solidarity—*absolutely*.

But nothing to warn her to take a step back, to make some wisecrack, or to clear her throat and utter something dampening to snap them both back to reality.

Maybe she'd been too busy living *all* the other emotions—the tension that had stretched throughout their meeting with Massimo, the rush of relief when they'd emerged on the street relatively unscathed. She'd felt scorched by the encounter, and she suspected the two men had as well, but none of them had been incinerated to the ground.

She'd been so grateful for that, and euphoric

in her relief. Ridiculously high that she'd even managed to make Lucas laugh.

That was why he'd kissed her—the shared laughter and euphoria, the relief; the realisation that he'd faced his worst fear and had survived. It had broken through his usual defences.

And she was kissing him back because she had no defences to rally against the rush of heat and yearning that gripped her. The achingly familiar feel of his lips on hers—fiery and exuberant...demanding—had her opening herself to him without restraint. She'd craved this man's touch for the past seven years. She had no thought of denying herself now.

With a groan, he gathered her close as if determined never to release her. As if he wanted to gorge himself on her. His heat and his scent surrounded her and she wrapped her arms around his neck and tried to crawl inside his skin and have all of him.

The sound of a phone's insistent ringing eventually broke into her consciousness. She stilled. So did Lucas. She opened her eyes to find him staring at her—a mix of emotions racing across his face. One she recognised with a nauseating jolt. *Horror.*

With a curse, he released her and took a step back.

Dragging in a breath, she tried to master the churning of her stomach, rallied her every resource. 'Okay.' They both ignored his ringing phone. 'Nobody is going to panic or say anything angry or cutting. Nobody is going to behave badly.'

His nostrils flared, but he gave a quick nod. 'Come, let's walk back to the boat. I don't think a drink now is a good idea.'

Damn it! They'd finally started to breathe easier around each other. She couldn't let one stupid kiss ruin that. A stupid and *heavenly* kiss.

She pushed that thought firmly from her mind. 'Okay, right. *That*—' she pointed back the way they'd come '—was just a moment.'

'A *moment*?' He glared at the path ahead, his hands clenching and unclenching. 'I should never have kissed you. It was—'

He said something in Italian she didn't understand, but it made her heart stutter. She'd thought all of his disgust and loathing had been aimed at her, but it was aimed at himself.

Reaching out, she pulled him to a halt. Nearby boat moorings jangled and a seabird let out a shrill cry.

He stared at her hand.

She released him, her heart thundering as if it were her own personal storm. 'Two things, Lucas. First of all, you don't need to worry that I'm going to misinterpret that kiss.'

Dark eyes throbbed into hers.

'I know you're not interested in starting anything romantic with me. I know that wasn't what that kiss was about.'

He didn't look relieved. If anything, his self-disgust only intensified. Did he hate himself for sending her mixed messages? Despite his initial bitterness when they'd first met again, he wasn't the kind of man who would deliberately raise her hopes just to dash them.

Maybe he loathed himself for his weakness in wanting her in the first place.

'It was just a silly moment.' She blew out a breath. 'We were so relieved that we'd escaped that interview in one piece that the sudden release in the tension took us off guard.'

'I still shouldn't—'

'And second, we're in a funny position, you and I. It sometimes feels as if we're in a bit of a time slip, where we're in the now times one moment and then suddenly hurtle back seven years ago. It's…disorienting.'

He opened his mouth, closed it again.

'It's probably normal. And it's probably normal to be—' the words that immediately popped to mind, words like *beguiled* and *seduced*, were far too suggestive '—taken off guard by it.' She shrugged with more confidence than she felt. 'But now that we're aware of it…'

'You've my assurance it won't happen again.'

He set off in the direction of their mooring at a quick clip and she had to trot to catch up.

His declaration should've made her feel better. Being on their guard and keeping their distance was the wisest course of action.

She recalled her long-ago miscarriage and swallowed. It was the *only* course of action. When she returned to the studio, she was pulling out her list. She'd study it with devoted ferocity. She needed to remind herself of all the reasons why she and Lucas could never be.

A meeting between Enrico and Massimo was arranged. After the initial contact, Enrico announced himself well pleased.

'Massimo is sorry for all of his past actions,' he told them, his smile wide. The smile slowly dissolved. 'He is living in penury.'

Hallie and Lucas exchanged a glance.

Enrico thumped the arm of his chair. 'He would not accept money!'

She straightened. He hadn't?

'He would not allow me to set him up in an apartment where he could be more comfortable. He says he is content where he is. *Pah*, that cannot be true!'

Lucas strode across to stare out a window. Hallie cleared her throat. 'He seemed content enough when we met him.'

'I can give him more! He is working for that charity—doing odd jobs, cleaning—in return for his board. But I—'

'He's doing something useful that makes him feel better about himself. Why would you take that away from him?'

Lucas turned to stare at her. The older man gave a disgruntled harrumph, before brightening again. 'I am going to take your advice and speak to Francesca and Rosa—they may wish to meet with him also.'

'Look at you, being all mature and adult,' she teased.

His eyes twinkled and he waggled a finger at her. 'You, miss, are a cheeky one.' He clapped his hands. 'Now come, do not keep an old man in suspense.' He eyed them like a dessert he was eager to sample. 'The two of you... If I am not mistaken, there is something still there, yes?'

She could feel herself colour. 'I...' Would it be better to be coy or not? She and Lucas hadn't discussed strategy beyond going on a few dates.

'I may be an old man, but I am not blind. I've seen the way you look at each other when you think no one is watching. I've seen the way you brighten when the other walks into the room. I see the way you get under each other's skin.'

They'd clearly been giving Oscar-worthy performances. Except...

Don't go there.

'I saw you dancing in the courtyard. Sparks were flying! You still care for each other. Still love each other, I think.'

She reached across and took Enrico's hands. 'It has been an unexpected joy to spend time with Lucas again, Enrico. But it is early days. You must not push. Leave us be to work things out.'

They needed to convince him to let them take things slowly. Especially if Lucas still wanted to go ahead with the fake engagement.

'*Pah*, where would you have been without me? I insisted you come here to Venice, did I not? I prompted Lucas to get you tickets to the opera. I knew he would take you shopping for something appropriate to wear. Did I not ask you to find Massimo?'

Her jaw dropped. Had that been a manipulation, too?

'Do not look at me like that! We do not know how much time I have left. What is wrong with me wanting to see you all happy and cared for?'

His bottom lip wobbled and unbidden tears burned her eyes. Lucas moved across and gripped Enrico's shoulder. 'Hallie is being understandably circumspect, Nonno.' He smiled down at the older man, and it was the kind of smile that had the power to turn a woman's heart over and over in her chest. 'But I do not think you need to have any fears where Hallie and I are concerned.'

The older man beamed at them both, clasping his hands beneath his chin. '*Carissima*, you make my heart full.'

Hallie hugged him before excusing herself, insisting she needed to get back to work.

So…were she and Lucas now supposed to hold hands whenever the family was together? Whisper sweet nothings in each other's ears? She gave a silent scream as she trudged up the stairs to her studio. *Kiss?* How on earth were they going to get through this?

A short time later Lucas tapped on the studio door. 'Can I come in?'

Setting her paintbrush down, she waved him in. Since that kiss—that ridiculously wonderful and ridiculously foolish kiss—Lucas had kept his distance. It was odd to discover she preferred his resentment and anger to this aloofness.

'I wanted to thank you.' He rubbed a hand over his nape. 'I don't know how you've done it, but you've helped smooth the way for this entire situation. And by entire situation I'm referring to both the Massimo thing as well as our pretend reconciliation. I'd have thought that impossible.'

She moved across to the sideboard and clicked on the electric kettle to make tea. 'That's mostly your doing, Lucas. You're the one who's put Enrico's wants and needs above your own.'

'You're being unnecessarily modest.'

'All I've done is keep things as pleasant as I can. If we want to look at it in black and white business terms,' which they *really* should, 'I'm being handsomely compensated to play my part.'

'You could've made things harder, but you've chosen not to. And I appreciate it.'

She made the tea. Handing him a mug, she hitched her head in the direction of the balcony, then settled into a chair. 'Enrico seems suitably chuffed with our…romantic developments.'

He sat beside her. 'More chuffed than you know.'

He rummaged around in his jacket pocket before bringing out a small velvet box and passing it across to her. 'I hope you haven't changed your mind about our fake engagement.'

Her mouth went dry. Inside the box was an engagement ring. The enormous emerald-cut diamond sparkled in the sunlight. 'Wow.' She blinked. 'That's, um…impressive.'

Was she supposed to put it on *now*?

One dark eyebrow rose as if surprised she wasn't at least a little dazzled. 'Are you saying you prefer your first engagement ring?'

Absolutely. A hundred times over. A thousand! She'd loved that little solitaire. To say as much, though, would be far too revealing.

'I couldn't have afforded something like this back then.'

Oh, Lord. How much did this rock cost?

Don't lose the ring, Hallie.

'After you left me and Enrico, I showed it to

him…told him I was going to propose. Naturally, he wanted to know when.'

'Naturally.' She wasn't entirely sure how she squeezed the word out. 'What did you tell him?'

'That I was waiting for the right moment.'

He glared at the scudding clouds racing across the sky. She rubbed at the spot above her heart, trying to ease an ache that had settled there. This was starting to feel like the most godawful sham. And *very* wrong.

'He, however, had a definite idea of when that ought to be.'

Keep things light. 'Of course he did. Hit me with it.'

His lips twisted into the semblance of a smile, though it didn't reach his eyes. 'He suggested the night of the opera.'

This Saturday night? She swallowed. 'Okay, then.'

Hallie handed him back the ring, as if glad to be free of it. Was she reluctant to do this? But back in February she agreed and—

Oh.

He slipped the velvet box back into his pocket. 'The ring is just a stage prop, Hallie, a mere frippery.'

'That's a big fat lie, Lucas Quinn.'

The way she called him out made him smile. 'What I'm trying to say in my clumsy way is that you don't need to be anxious wearing it. It doesn't matter if you lose it.'

Those opal eyes flashed. 'I won't be losing that ring, Lucas. You *will* be getting it back at the end of all of this.'

'You could keep it. Consider it a bonus for—'

'You'll be getting the ring back!'

He blinked at her sharpness.

She scowled at the building opposite, before blowing out a breath and rolling her shoulders. 'The dresses, though, are all mine.'

She sent him a small smile and his jaw unclenched at the mischief that laced its edges. He wasn't sure how she did it—how she could so easily smooth an awkward moment. He chuckled. 'That's probably just as well. I don't think they'll fit me.'

They sipped their tea silently for a bit. 'So here's a question for you,' he said, keen to move the conversation on from their impending engagement. 'Don't you think it's odd that I can't seem to find it in me to hate Massimo?' The question had been burning through him for days.

He felt the weight of her gaze, but didn't turn his head to meet it.

'I don't know.' From the corner of his eye he saw her shrug. 'It's kind of hard to hate the man we met the other day.'

He shifted on his chair. 'I'm not saying I don't condemn his past actions.'

'Never thought that for a moment.'

She knew him too well. Still. Even after all these years. It ought to send alarm bells clanging through him, but it didn't. It brought a strange kind of peace instead.

A gondola slid silently by on the canal below, the passengers' faces lit with excitement. Someone waved to Hallie when they glanced up and saw her watching. She waved back, her lips curving into a generous grin.

When was the last time he'd felt excited about anything? When was the last time something as simple as a stranger's wave had made him smile? What was the point of all his money if he had nothing to look forward to?

What the hell...? He shook the thought off. Though speaking of excitement... 'Seeing Massimo has brought Enrico such joy. I can't begrudge him that.'

Hallie turned back. 'Your grandfather has a heart big enough for everyone. As for Massimo...' She chewed on her bottom lip. 'As long as he keeps his word and doesn't take advantage of Enrico then I suppose that reflects well on him.'

He frowned. 'Yeah.'

Her gaze didn't drop from his. 'You don't have to like him, you know? And you don't have to trust him.'

'But I don't have to hate him, which is a revelation.' He drained the last of his tea. 'It's thrown me for a loop.' He suspected his lack of acrimony was due to Hallie's influence, and that left him all at sea, too.

'We imagined worst-case scenarios and terrible outcomes when we first approached him. We thought he'd behave badly and hurt Enrico, take advantage of him. Maybe this is a symptom of our relief that none of that has happened. Though, it's still early days. I won't be letting my guard down just yet.'

Her words made him want to hug her. 'You know what keeps playing around and around in my mind? The fact you initially refused Enrico's request to find Massimo. Because you didn't want to lie to me.' He set down his mug. 'I'd behaved so badly. I didn't deserve that kind of consideration from you.'

She stiffened. 'You didn't *not* deserve it. And betraying you like that would've been a terrible thing to do.'

He was silent for a long moment. 'I'd forgotten how kind you were.'

Her mouth fell open.

'Thank you, Hallie. Thank you for remaining true to your own moral code and not allowing my bitterness to infect you.'

The opera was the kind of torture he wouldn't wish on his worst enemy. Hallie wore her emerald-green gown and glowed as brightly and brilliantly as a jewel herself. When she'd glided down the stairs to the living room where he'd been waiting for her, he hadn't been able to drag his gaze away. Which was just as well with Enrico watching and the pretence they were enacting.

Hallie had been careful to keep her gaze trained on him, a soft secret smile curving luscious lips. He'd had to remind himself this was all for show. It didn't mean anything.

That didn't stop the entire surface of his skin tightening with a burning, prickling heat whenever he looked at her, though. So he did his best not to look at her. He couldn't resist a glance when he led her to their box at the Teatro la Fenice—the theatre was one of the most famous landmarks in the city. Her lips parted as she took in the stucco and gold, the painted ceiling and the overwhelming grandeur of it all. 'Oh, Lucas,' she'd breathed.

It was all he could do not to swoop down and kiss her. Gritting his teeth, he took her wrap and helped her to her seat—outwardly the perfect gentleman, but inside a ravenous beast raged. Clenching his jaw, he counted to ten.

He couldn't concentrate on the performance, but he was attuned to every thrill that rippled through the woman beside him. In the interval she stared at him, dazed, saying, 'This is the most amazing experience. Thank you, Lucas. I sense this may not be your favourite way to spend an evening, though, so I really do appreciate it.'

Hold on. *What?*

She wrinkled her nose. 'You've not exactly been spellbound.'

Oh, he was. Just not by the opera.

'I hope you're not finding it too tiresome or boring.'

'Not at all.' The evening might be challenging and frustrating, but it was far from boring. 'I apologise if I haven't been attentive. I've had a lot on my mind.'

She sipped her champagne and remained silent after that.

In the inside pocket of his jacket, that little velvet box burned like a broken promise. And a disaster waiting to happen. When he'd embarked on this pretence, he hadn't considered the ethics of what he was asking of Hallie. Or himself. At the time, all he'd cared about was giving Enrico peace and joy during his final months.

But feigning such a commitment—one that ought to be sacrosanct—now felt morally questionable.

They had a drink afterwards in a sumptuous bar that would make a great location for a fake wedding proposal. He didn't even need to actually propose—he just needed to hand her the ring. No matter how much he told himself to do exactly that, he couldn't seem to do it.

They puttered home and it was as he was tying the boat to the mooring that Hallie's phone rang.

Blinking, she pulled it from her purse, her brows shooting up when she read the caller ID. 'My father,' she whispered, before pressing it to her ear. 'Dad?'

If Lucas had been asked to describe Hallie's relationship with her father in one word, he'd have chosen *dutiful*. As far as he could see, though, most of the duty rested on Hallie's side. In the three years he and Hallie had been together, Lucas had never even met the man. Simon hadn't visited his daughter in London. Not even when he'd been in Europe for a conference. Not even after she'd announced their engagement.

Dr Simon Alexander was a cancer research specialist with a list of letters behind his name as long as his arm. According to Hallie, he'd always been wedded to his work. To the detriment of both his wife and child.

In the final year that he and Hallie had been together, Lucas had known she'd been drawing connections between him and Simon. He'd sworn to her more than once, though, that as soon as the company was safe from the circling sharks, his workload would decrease drastically.

The wary expression on her face as she spoke to her father now, though, had him frowning. Why hadn't he paid more attention to her fears back then? Had he been blinded by his own single-minded ambition?

'What?'

Hallie went pale and her hands started to shake. Lucas was at her side in seconds. With his hand at her elbow, he led her inside the palazzo and guided her down to a chaise longue, easing down beside her. Her hand gripped his as if her life depended on it.

She nodded at whatever her father said. 'Yes, of course,' she croaked. 'I'm sorry you've had to deal with all of that.' Her gaze lifted to Lucas's and he sucked in a breath at the shadows in her eyes, and then his own phone rang and she immediately released him, eased fractionally away.

He pulled out his phone, a hard knot tightening his chest when he recognised the number of his real estate agent in Sydney. He listened in silence as the agent gave him the same information Hallie's father had no doubt just imparted to her—that there'd been a fire in the building that housed her studio.

He closed his eyes. All her beautiful paintings? Her equipment? 'How bad is the damage?'

Apparently still being assessed was the reply.

Ending the call, he crouched down in front of her. 'I'm so very sorry, Hallie. Are you okay?'

'Dad says it's a big mess. That it's…' Her bottom lip wobbled, but she pushed her shoulders back, removed her hands from his. 'Never mind.

Nobody was hurt in the fire and that's the main thing.'

'A blessing, yes.' But what of her beautiful artworks? All her years of hard work? All of the memories the studio must hold? A roar sounded through him. He'd promised her that building and while it made no sense, he felt as if he'd let her down.

'What else did your father say?'

She stared at her hands. 'That he has an important conference coming up and doesn't have time to deal with the insurance company or the clean-up. I need to go home and take care of it.' One slim shoulder lifted. 'Maybe there are things that can be salvaged.'

Her pallor caught at him. She glanced around as if all at sea. He took both of her hands again and urged her to look at him. 'I'll organise us flights for as soon as possible.'

'Us?'

He squeezed her hands. 'You don't have to face this alone.' He dreaded the sight that would greet her when she returned. If her father refused to be there for her then Lucas would be.

'I know you're busy—'

'Not too busy for this.' He stood. 'And I've a vested interest, if you recall.'

She shook herself as if she'd forgotten that detail. 'Of course.' Her brow pleated. 'I'm sorry about your investment, Lucas. I—'

'That's the least of my worries. What we need to do is see if we can salvage anything from your studio.'

She stared at him and eventually nodded. 'It'll be nice not to be on my own. Thank you.'

When they landed in Sydney, they drove straight to the studio. He knew she wouldn't rest until she'd seen the damage for herself. Neither would he. Though he'd insist she have a decent meal and a sleep afterwards.

He'd been sent the incident report. The fire was the result of an electrical fault. The structural damage was minor—the building safe to enter—but there was extensive fire and water damage to the contents of the studio as well as the shops downstairs.

Stepping inside, they both sucked in a breath. The studio was a damp blackened mess. Lucas barely recognised it as the same place he'd visited in February. Hallie sifted through some of the debris, her eyes widening with disbelief. 'It's even worse than I imagined.'

Her shoulders began to shake. In two strides he was at her side and had her in his arms. He held her close as she cried, fighting the lump in his throat as he stared around at the damage.

Eventually, her crying stopped and she eased away, dragging a hand over her eyes, leaving behind a sooty smudge in its wake. 'I'm sorry. I…'

'Nothing to apologise for. I feel like howling myself.'

'It's all such a mess, Lucas. I don't even know where to start. I doubt there's anything to salvage.'

'Not true,' he said, spying a familiar figure amongst the debris and swooping down to claim it. 'He might be looking a little worse for wear but Trevor has survived the blaze.' He lifted the cast-iron rooster aloft.

She gave a shaky laugh. 'Way to go, Trev.' Taking him, she hugged him to her chest.

She looked done in. She needed a shower, a hot meal and a decent sleep. 'Do you trust me, Hallie?'

Her gaze returned to his. 'I…' She frowned. 'Yes.'

'Then let me take care of everything. Let me organise a salvage crew to make a start on this. I promise no major decisions will be made without your go-ahead.'

'I…'

'I'd like to help.'

Her shoulders sagged. 'I'd really appreciate that.'

'In the meantime, how about we head to your flat and freshen up. I for one need a decent cup of coffee and a change of clothes.'

He'd take her home, ensure she had a proper meal and then insist she lie down for a bit. Then he'd get to work on all that needed doing. He'd organise a salvage company to work around the clock until the job was done.

He hadn't meant to let her down seven years ago, but he'd started to see all the ways he had. This time he wouldn't. This time he'd do whatever she needed doing.

CHAPTER TEN

LUCAS PERFORMED MIRACLES. He had a salvage crew at the site on the afternoon of their arrival and oversaw everything. But not even all of his hard work and resources could counter the loss.

Hallie was grateful she'd had the foresight to store her unfinished commissions in a climate-controlled storage facility. To lose those would've been devastating. Nevertheless, the loss of her own artworks and all of her equipment hit her hard. As did losing personal items like diaries, commendations, letters and awards. She did her best to keep a stiff upper lip, but there were inevitable tears. Lucas was a rock throughout all of it.

His presence was reassuring and comforting. And confusing.

Of course he cared. He wasn't a monster. He'd feel bad for anyone in the same situation. It was just that this felt more…personal.

While they'd become more friendly in recent weeks, they weren't friends. Or were they? No matter how often she told herself not to read too much into it, she couldn't help hoping...

What? What did she hope for? She had to stop being such a sap. Lucas was probably just interested in minimising the collateral damage to his investment. This building *was* part of their arrangement. Now that it was damaged he might be worried she'd renege on their deal and leave him in the lurch.

Her throat tightened. But surely he wouldn't think that of her, would he?

See? *Confusing!*

Along with the losses, though, there were unexpected wins. Like discovering one of her art school sketchbooks had survived deep inside a forgotten drawer. Finding her very first art prize—a palette and paintbrush trophy that she'd won at the age of eleven—tucked away beneath a pile of ashes in a protected corner. After a good scrub and touch-up with a little paint, Trevor looked as good as new. Small things, and all the more precious for thinking them lost for ever, discovered like jewels amid the soot and ruin.

Most of the clean-up was accomplished in a week. Lucy, Dorothy and William from the shops downstairs thanked her profusely when they saw her, and that was when she learnt that Lucas had organised salvage crews for them as well. His thoughtfulness touched her, but he'd waved away her thanks. 'I wanted to help, and I'm lucky enough to be in a position to do so.'

Luck had nothing to do with it. Lucas's success was down to hard work, determination and his canny business acumen. None of his many successes had fallen into his lap. He'd made them happen.

Surveying him late one afternoon after they'd made their way back to her flat from the studio, she noted the tired lines fanning out from his eyes and the grim line of his mouth. He looked exhausted. Had she been leaning on him too hard?

She bit her lip. 'Is the bed in the spare room okay?' When she'd offered it to him on Thursday he'd accepted. She'd been glad of the company, but maybe he'd have been more comfortable elsewhere—like a five-star hotel. Her flat was comfortable, but it wasn't large, and it certainly wasn't luxurious like the palazzo in Venice.

He glanced up. 'Very comfortable. Why?'

'Just checking.' She glanced at the report he was reading and frowned. 'Are you actually getting any sleep?'

He set it down. 'You're worried I'm working when I should be sleeping?'

Was he? 'Are you?'

'I'm not. But I would like you to spit out whatever it is you have on your mind.'

He didn't say it unkindly so she did. 'I'm wor-

ried that sorting my studio out has taken prece-
dence when you've other claims on your time. I
promise that you don't need to go to those kinds
of lengths. I'm not going to withdraw from our
deal.'

Two tiny frown lines appeared between his
eyes. 'Hallie—'

'I care about Enrico and I want—'

'Hallie!'

She broke off.

'Stop worrying.' He tapped a finger to the
report. 'This is just me keeping my eye in. The
company mostly runs without me these days.
Nothing is being neglected. I just didn't want
you dealing with all of this on your own.'

He rubbed a hand over his face. 'I can imagine what it would be like to lose my home. And
I can imagine even more clearly what it would
be like to lose my life's work. Nobody should
have to face that devastation alone.'

So…? He was doing this for *her*?

She ignored the way her heart lifted. It didn't
change the fact that he looked tired and worn.
He'd been wholly present for her these past few
days, and if she'd ever needed proof that he'd
have kept his words seven years ago, she had it
now in spades.

If only you'd waited.

A part of her wished with all her might that
she had. She did her best to ignore it. What

they'd lost could never be regained, and pining for it was pointless. She'd have had to be a different person back then, someone not haunted by her mother's despair and her father's emotional remoteness. The person she'd been then would've held Lucas back, and he'd deserved to fly free to scale the heights of success that he'd craved.

'Hallie, is everything okay?'

He was doing all of this *for her.* So far, though, exhaustion had been his only reward. 'Vegetables.' She clapped her hands. They'd start with the basics. 'I need vegetables.' She smiled, and he blinked. 'We've been eating too much takeaway.'

She pointed at his report. 'So you catch up on what you need to, while I duck to the shops. And then I'm going to cook a stir-fry while dancing to really loud music. Consider yourself warned.'

His answering smile chased some of the shadows from his eyes.

Over the stir-fry that evening, she asked, 'How many times have you been to Sydney?'

He held up two fingers as he wolfed down the food she'd set in front of him. He pointed to it. 'This is great.'

'So…your first time was in February?' When he'd bid on her portrait sketch?

'I was only here for three nights.'

Talk about a flying trip. 'Did you see anything of the city?'

'My hotel room, the ballroom where the gala dinner was held and your studio.'

Her fork clattered to her plate.

'But I saw the harbour when we flew in on Tuesday morning. It was a heck of a sight.'

'Okay, that's it. We're going sightseeing tomorrow.'

'We're…?'

'Sydney is beautiful, Lucas. You have to see some of it firsthand. And you're lucky enough to have a local as your tour guide.'

He blinked.

She metaphorically dusted off her hands. 'It'll do the both of us good. I've hovered around the studio enough for one week. My presence hasn't been helping, though everyone has been far too polite to point that out. It's time to get out from underfoot and let people get on with their work.'

He pointed his fork at her. 'Not underfoot.'

'Underfoot,' she repeated. She'd been worrying at all the things, prodding at them like a tongue at a sore tooth. It was time to stop wallowing. Her lovely mum had wallowed and it had done her no good. It was time for Hallie to start counting her blessings instead.

The next day they caught the train into the city and strolled through the Botanic Gardens beside the harbour, stopping off to sit in Mrs Macquarie's chair with its extraordinary view. The sun shone with a gratifying enthusiasm and a light breeze rippled the bay, making the water sparkle as if lit by hundreds of tiny suns. Sydney looked its very best.

Lifting her face to the sky, Hallie closed her eyes and dragged in the scent of sea air and roses. *Thank you, Sydney.* When she opened them again, she found Lucas staring at her. Her heart did a funny bumpety-bump. She tried to cover it up by gesturing at the view. 'It's something, isn't it?'

'Amazing,' he agreed, releasing her from his gaze. 'It's bigger than I imagined. And busier. And the light here is so *bright.*'

They continued around to Circular Quay. His hands went to his hips and he simply stared when they reached the Opera House. She ordered coffee so he could drink in the view... and she could drink in the sight of him finally starting to relax.

'Your city is beautiful.'

The appreciation in his eyes had her wanting to hug herself. And him.

You're not hugging anyone.

They jumped on a ferry to Watsons Bay and ate seafood at a tiny waterside restaurant that she told him was one of Sydney's best-kept secrets.

They laughed and chatted over delicious seafood, and the shadows in his eyes retreated even further. Which left her feeling unaccountably chuffed. When his gaze lifted at the precise moment she studied him so closely, catching her unawares, something arced between them. Something hot and sweet.

Swallowing, he pointed to the blackboard. 'I understand pavlova is a feted Australian dessert, but the macadamia tart sounds tempting.'

The pulse at the base of his jaw pounded, and her heart lodged in her throat. The attraction between them had been dormant, on hold while they'd dealt with the shock of the fire, but it flared back to full-bodied life now. If possible, it had grown in intensity. Trying to hide it was becoming increasingly difficult.

You're an adult. You can do this.

Reaching for what she hoped was a nonchalant shrug, she said, 'Let's get one of each and share them.'

They spent the afternoon exploring The Rocks, where he bought souvenirs for everyone back home, before joining the crowds in the city and window shopping just for fun. Before they headed home she bought a collection of local cheeses, cured meats and fancy olives for a grazing platter for dinner. Along with a nice bottle of Australian wine.

'Did you achieve whatever you set out to

achieve today?' Lucas asked over the food later that evening.

Feigning ignorance, she topped up his wineglass with a very nice Shiraz from the Hunter Valley. If he was staying in Australia longer she could take him the two-hour drive north to explore the vineyards. That'd be fun. 'What do you mean?'

'There was a reason you took me sightseeing today. I'm curious to know if you achieved your objective.'

She searched his face, but all she found there was curiosity. 'You've done so much for me, and I wanted to thank you. I thought it might be a nice treat to see some of the sights before you headed home.'

'And that's all?'

'What else would there be?'

One broad shoulder lifted. 'I had a feeling last night that there was something more to it.'

Had he not enjoyed himself? Had…? 'Were you *humouring* me?' Is that what today had been about?

'No! Today was… It was a perfect day, Hallie. I just thought…' He trailed off. 'Never mind, I was mistaken.'

'Fine! Not mistaken,' she grumbled. This man was too perceptive by half. Blowing out a breath, she wrinkled her nose. 'Yesterday afternoon I glanced across and you looked…'

He raised an eyebrow.

'Exhausted. When I asked if you were sleeping okay you said you were, and when I asked if you were working too hard you said that you weren't. Which is when I realised *I* was the reason you looked so tired.'

He froze in the act of reaching for a piece of smoked cheddar.

'You've been worried about me *and* dealing with the salvage crew single-handedly. I've been so self-involved I hadn't noticed. I feel bad about that. I'm sorry I've been leaning on you so hard.'

'*You* have nothing to feel bad about.'

He shot to his feet and started pacing around her small living room. She uncurled her feet from under her and set them on the floor.

'Your father hasn't been to see you once since we arrived.'

What did her father have to do with anything? 'I told you we weren't close.'

'Has he even phoned you?'

Once, but only to ensure the insurance company knew he was no longer their point of contact. She didn't think Lucas wanted to hear about that.

'He's treated you like this your entire life?'

For her father, work was everything. She often wondered why he'd ever married. 'I've long given up hope that he'll change.'

'But your mother didn't.'

Air left her body in a rush, as if a roller coaster had whooshed her down a steep incline at a lightning-fast pace, leaving her lungs behind.

'And that's what you saw every day of your life. Your mother constantly waiting for your father to see her, to find some time for her, to show her some affection.'

Her eyes burned.

'And when it didn't happen she became more and more heartbroken. I remember you telling me about it. I remember feeling sad for her. But it didn't hit me, until I was here, what that must've looked like to you.'

Her heart pounded in jagged leaps.

'Seven years ago I didn't understand how you could draw comparisons between me and your father. I was offended by them. I didn't understand how afraid you must've been of history repeating. I should've recognised the gravity of your fears rather than feeling wounded by what I saw as your lack of faith in us…in *me*.'

She opened her mouth to say something— *anything*…

'I'm exhausted, Hallie, because it's grim work coming face-to-face with reality and recognising the ways in which I failed you.'

She shot to her feet. 'Oh, please, Lucas, don't do this. Hindsight is a double-edged sword. We both made mistakes back then. We shouldn't judge our younger selves based on what we know now. We did the best we could at the time. And we've achieved things we should be proud of. That's not so bad, is it?'

Her words didn't ease the steel from his spine. His hands clenched and unclenched. 'Being here has made me see things differently. I can see now why our baby meant so much to you, why you wanted it so badly, why creating a family mattered so much to you.'

She took a step away from him. She couldn't talk about this.

'Hallie—' agonised eyes met hers '—I can't let you keep thinking that I didn't care about our child or that I didn't love it. I did. I just didn't realise how much until it was too late.'

Her heart pounded like a hammer. She could feel her every atom pulsing with the force of it.

'I felt guilty about that—for letting my worries overshadow the joy. In a screwed-up way it made me think I wasn't entitled to my grief. Not in the same way you were entitled to yours.'

She wanted to run. Or yell. But her legs wouldn't work and she couldn't push a single syllable from her throat.

'I certainly had no intention of burdening you with it, though. You were going through hell and I wanted to support you, do what I could to help you.'

He'd loved...?

'I thought knowing how I felt would weigh

you down, add to your grief. I didn't understand back then that sharing my grief would've made both of us feel less alone. I'm sorry for that. Deeply sorry.'

He'd loved...?

Stepping forward, she planted her hands either side of his face. 'Do you mean that?' She searched his eyes fiercely.

He stared back, his face raw and ragged, not trying to hide anything. 'I loved our unborn baby,' he said as if sensing she needed to hear him say it again. 'I wish with all my heart the pregnancy had gone full term.'

She released him, her palms burning from the intriguing scrape of his stubble, even as the rest of her felt lighter. 'You really *loved* our baby.'

He nodded.

'I thought you were relieved when I miscarried.'

He looked stricken and tears welled, making everything blur. 'I thought you considered my pregnancy as just another thing to worry about. A burden.' She wondered now how—after seeing him with the Zaneris—she could've ever thought that of him. 'So when I miscarried, I thought you were relieved.' But...

He'd *loved* their unborn baby.

He thumbed away a tear that slid down her cheek, and then another one, and shook his head.

'I was gutted. And I hid it from you. Because I was an idiot.'

Because he'd been protective. 'When you kept telling me we'd have children in the future, I thought it meant you figured they'd replace the one we'd lost.'

'That was my clumsy attempt to give you hope. Seems dumb now. I knew nothing would replace the baby we'd lost.'

'I'm sorry,' she said on a sob.

'God, Hallie, please don't cry.'

Gathering her in his arms, he held her against his chest until she'd pulled herself together. Resisting the warmth that tried to steal over her, she eased away.

He stared down at her, his eyes dark with concern. 'Okay?'

She nodded. Some awful broken place inside her had started to heal at the realisation that he'd loved their baby, too. The past rejigged into a slightly different shape. A better shape.

He shrugged, gave a funny half-grimace half-smile. 'In my mind I've always imagined we'd have had a little green-eyed girl with strawberry blonde hair.'

Her lips trembled. 'While I imagined a little dark-haired, dark-eyed boy.'

They both smiled stupidly at each other for a moment, but then his expression sobered. 'I missed that baby. And when you left, I missed you, too, Hallie. Every single day.'

The intensity, the attraction, the need, flared between them. In an instant. Just like that. Between heartbeats. It wrapped around her in seductive arcs like silk and smoke, and stronger than steel.

The words slipped out of him, a simple statement of fact. He hadn't meant them to. He ought to find a way to recall them, make light of them, infer it all belonged to a long-ago past. But he couldn't manage logical thought above the roaring in his ears. Hallie stared at him as if she'd like to drag him into her bedroom and have her wicked way with him.

'Same.' Her chin lifted. 'When I heard your voice at the gala dinner, I spent the rest of the night lecturing myself how to behave, ordering myself to act like a grown-up.'

The pounding of his heart took up the same beat as the pulse throbbing at the base of her throat. 'You thought you'd be angry with me, the way I was angry with you. That you'd have to hide it, hold it in.' She'd done an excellent job.

'I was afraid I'd kiss you. For seven years, I *dreamed* of kissing you.'

His skin tightened and heat gathered in his veins. He swore, though it sounded like a caress.

'I never felt more alive than when I was kissing you, Lucas.'

Had she stepped closer or had he?

'And I want to kiss you now—so badly—but maybe that's the last thing you want.'

'Hallie.' Her name was a gasp, a groan.

Her gaze raked his face and her eyes widened and her lips parted as if she could see his hunger reflected there. She pulled in a breath, as if starved of air. 'But if we kiss we might not want to stop, which is fine with me—better than fine—but I want you to be okay with that, too. I don't want you waking up in the morning regretting it. I—'

'Dream come true,' he enunciated clearly. He'd be every bit as honest as her. 'Dream come true.'

She reached out and touched him then. The heat of her hand on his chest burned fire through him. The way she sucked in a breath told him she felt exactly the same. 'I don't know where any of this will lead.'

Him, either. He only knew that if he didn't kiss her soon he'd die. 'We don't have to make any promises.' Not yet. In this moment they were just two people who'd dropped all pretence, who'd given up trying to hide their need for one another.

His hands curved around her shoulders, his head lowering towards hers. She swayed closer, her lips parting and their breaths mingling. 'Lucas?'

His name was a whispered plea that had the base of his spine tingling and tightening. 'Yes?' When her hand curved around his neck, the skin-on-skin contact had him hissing in a breath.

'Please tell me you have protection.'

He nodded.

She became a primal siren then, turning more fully into him, her fingers ruffling through the thick hair at his nape, urging his head down to hers.

His mouth moved to within a whisper's breath of hers and he held them there for a moment, on the cusp, and her lips curved as it relishing the moment, too. The anticipation built until his world shrank to nothing but her and the desire streaking through his every pore.

When he finally allowed his lips to touch hers, he'd meant for the kiss to be gentle—a slow wooing, unlike that day outside the monastery where he'd fallen on her like an uncouth teenager. But Hallie had other ideas. Her open-mouthed kiss and the teasing sweep of her tongue against his lips demanded more, demanded everything, as if she wanted all of him immediately, as if she was so starved that nothing but everything would now suffice. The thought was so intoxicating he drowned in it, kissing her with a roaring need that made her gasp and try to crawl inside his skin.

'Shirt!' She tugged at it. 'Needs to go,' she panted.

He eased far enough away to drag the polo shirt over his head. 'Dress,' he growled back.

Reaching behind, she unzipped her sundress and let it pool at her feet. His mouth went dry. She stood in front of him in a silky half-cup bra in the palest pink and a tiny scrap of matching silk parading as panties. If he'd known that was all she'd been wearing beneath her dress all day he'd have not been able to focus on anything else. Titian's *Venus*, his favourite painting, had nothing on the sight that met his eyes now.

She glanced at his jeans and raised an eyebrow. He eased them down his thighs and stepped out of them, his erection pressing against the material of his briefs. She stared, her cheeks flushing pink and her teeth sinking into her bottom lip as if she couldn't wait to unwrap the rest of him. She made him feel as beautiful as Michelangelo's *David*. Reaching back down, he extracted a row of foil condoms from his wallet, before letting the wallet drop back to the floor.

Planting a hand in the middle of his chest, she pushed him backwards in the direction of her bedroom, her eyes gleaming. Cold marble fled and he became putty. Heat and putty.

When the backs of his legs hit her bed, he fell backwards onto it and she followed him down. Straddling his thighs and holding his gaze, she unclasped her bra, eased it down her arms and threw it behind her. .

His hands shook as they lifted to cup her breasts. He'd dreamed of this—would wake in the middle of the night in a fevered sweat, loss pounding through him when he realised he'd only been dreaming. But this was real, and he meant to cherish every moment.

His thumbs brushed against taut nipples and she arched into him with a soft cry. Her entire frame shook. He gritted his teeth when she pressed herself against the thick hardness of his erection. If he wasn't careful he'd disgrace himself. And he wanted to draw out her pleasure, make it last, to savour every last drop, before making her come again and again.

Wrapping an arm around her waist, he rolled them over, taking his weight on his forearms. Her breathy laugh brushed across the skin of his throat, and her hands traced the lines of his shoulders. He captured her mouth in another soul-drugging kiss, before working his way down her throat until he could capture the peak of one breast in his mouth and lathe it with his tongue. Her cry sang through his veins. He gave his full attention to her breasts until she writhed beneath him. His name on her lips.

Only then did he continue a path down her body. He wanted—

'Lucas!'

He froze at the command in her voice.

Reaching down she seized his shoulders and dragged him back up until they were eye to eye. 'I want you too much to wait.'

'But I—'

Taking his hand, she guided it down between her thighs—to her heat and her wetness. He went so hard and tight he thought he might burst. He circled a finger around her sensitive nub before dipping a finger inside her. Her body arched up to meet him. 'See?' She gasped. 'I'm ready—'

She broke off with a half sob when his fingers continued their ministrations.

When her hand slid beneath his briefs to circle his hardness, it was his turn to bite back a moan.

'Lucas.' His name was a moan of pure need.

'Tell me what you want.' He'd move heaven and earth to give it to her.

'I want to feel you between my thighs and inside me, filling me.'

Stars burst behind his eyelids.

'I want to feel connected to you. At one with you.'

Her words pierced an armour he hadn't known he still had. It shattered into shards all around him.

'And then I want to lose myself to pleasure.' She swallowed. 'If that's okay with you.'

Okay? It was—

'I promise to give you whatever you want next time.'

There'd be a next time?

'If you want,' she whispered, and he realised he'd said the words out loud. 'I hope so. Don't you?'

'So much it ought to frighten me.'

But there was no room for fear when he was touching her so intimately and with his body so on fire for her. Gritting his teeth he eased away, dragging that silly scrap of silk down her legs, and shucking his briefs. He reached for a foil packet then sheathed himself with a condom.

She watched with bright, hungry eyes. Coming back to her, covering her body with his, he brushed the hair from her face. Maintaining eye contact, he pushed gently at her entrance. She angled her hips and they slid together in a gentle rush. A sigh escaped her and her eyelids fluttered closed. 'Bliss,' she whispered, opening her eyes again.

A strange joy gripped him.

Flinging her head back, she wrapped her thighs around his waist, her body arching up to meet his. 'You feel like heaven, Lucas.'

And then they were moving together, their movements perfectly in sync like they were dancing, until he couldn't work out where she started and he ended. Their movements grew more urgent, their rhythm a passionate, inexorable tattoo thrumming in his blood, and in hers. With a cry, her body bowed and lifted, pulsing and vibrating against his. He had no defence against hot, sweet muscles clenching around his hardness. With a cry, he, too, spiralled over the edge into a vortex of pleasure.

He hadn't known that a single act of lovemaking could have such an impact. Holding Hallie cradled against him afterwards, Lucas chose not to question it.

No promises had been made, and although seven years' worth of misunderstandings lay between them, it felt as if somehow—and despite all the odds—they'd found their way back to one another.

Crazy? Perhaps.

Fate? Perhaps.

Wishful thinking? Maybe.

But as he fell into a drowsy sleep, he couldn't help feeling as if the world had just opened up to him in a new and better way.

CHAPTER ELEVEN

HALLIE DIDN'T IMMEDIATELY open her eyes when she woke the following morning. She could sense Lucas beside her and she needed to steel herself before opening them and meeting his gaze. She didn't know what she'd do if he regretted last night.

Turning her head on the pillow, she found him watching her with a wry smile. 'I was wondering how long it'd take for you to open your eyes.'

His smile was easy and his eyes clear. It was as if she'd been hurtled back seven years. There was no awkwardness and no need for pretence. She rolled fully to her side to face him, tucked her hands beneath her cheek. 'I was girding my loins in case you regretted last night, but...'

'I don't,' he said.

A funny fluttering lifted through her, like a thousand butterflies taking flight into a shaft of sunlight. 'Last night was something, huh?'

One side of his mouth hooked up. 'Understatement much? Hallie, last night was off the charts.'

They grinned at each other. After they'd woken from that first explosive coming together, they'd made love again—slowly and leisurely... and every bit as gloriously. And then the third time had been a playful rediscovery of one another.

Propping his head on his elbow, he stared down at her. 'What would you like to do today?'

Stay in bed all day. With him.

His mouth hooked up into one of those lop-sided grins, as if he'd read her mind, and a sigh of appreciation gathered beneath her breastbone. 'I'd love to sketch you looking like this.'

He shrugged. 'Okay.'

He'd always been generous like that—letting her sketch him whenever she wanted. He'd once told her that watching her become absorbed was mesmerising, and that in sketching him she made him feel seen. That he'd loved the calm, the connection and the peace. Of course, that had been before he'd started his own company. After that, there'd been no time for long, lazy afternoons or slow weekend mornings.

He's not that man any more.

'Right, don't move a muscle.' After leaping out of bed, she shrugged on her robe before grabbing her sketchpad and a pencil.

'I have a condition, though. You can only sketch me...'

She swung around.

'If you're naked, too.'

She let her robe fall back to the floor.

The next three days passed in an enchanted haze. Encased in their own little bubble, the rest of the world retreated. What remained was the two of them, fun and laughter and lazy nights making love. They avoided talking about what it meant, avoided discussing the future; they made no promises. It was too soon. But it felt as if the future bloomed ahead of them like something precious and rare. And auspicious.

She took him swimming in the cold surf and for long cliff walks beside the churning sea. They held hands and fed each other fish and chips. They even went to a rock festival in the park one night where they danced until they were breathless. And then they went home to her flat and made love until they were even more breathless.

Lucas's phone rang and Hallie cracked open an eyelid to peer at the clock—five a.m.—and suppressed a groan.

'Rosa.' Lucas rolled to his back, not bothering to suppress his. 'Do you know what time it is?'

Rosa still hadn't mastered the time difference. It was why Lucas was the one who usually rang for the daily update on Enrico.

She sensed his tension before he shot upright in bed. 'He's…'

She sat up, too, suddenly and fully awake. 'And how is he now?'

Enrico. She held her breath as Lucas listened to the answer.

'I'll be on the first plane I can get out of here.' He ended the call and turned to Hallie, breathing hard. 'Enrico has been rushed to hospital.'

'Oh, Lucas.' The shadows in his eyes had her fighting tears. Reaching out, she squeezed his hand. 'What else did Rosa say?'

'That they've stabilised him for the moment, but still consider his condition serious.' He flung back the covers and leapt out of bed. 'I shouldn't have lingered here so long, enjoying myself. Not when Enrico—'

'Stop!' Leaping out of bed, too, she raced around and stood in front of him. 'Enrico thinks we're on the brink of announcing our engagement. He expected you to come to Australia with me. *That* made him happy. It would've looked odd if you'd remained behind. You don't have anything to feel guilty about.'

Dragging a hand through his hair, he nodded. 'I need to go back now, though. *Pronto.*'

She pointed to the phone, still clutched in his hand. 'You make a plane reservation and I'll start packing your things.'

He immediately started punching in numbers

on his phone while she charged into the spare bedroom and seized his suitcase.

'Did you get a flight?' she asked when he appeared in the doorway.

He nodded, looking utterly exhausted, and utterly lost.

'Am I returning with you?'

'No.'

The single word felt like a slap. 'But—'

'I could only get one seat. Once we know how Enrico is doing, I'll send you word and we'll organise your return to Venice then. In the meantime, perhaps you could oversee the building repairs?'

'Don't worry about any of that,' she said, shaking her head.

She went with him to the airport. He'd gone so silent, so distant, as if the past few days hadn't happened…as if they hadn't meant anything. She told herself not to take it to heart. He was consumed with worry for the grandfather he adored.

The thing was there hadn't been enough time yet to consolidate whatever had grown between them, to work out what their relationship had evolved into, or to give it any kind of label. It was too early for cold, hard realities. And a tiny part of her couldn't help wondering if he blamed her for having kept him away for so long from his grandfather.

His haggard expression, the way he twitched and fidgeted, caught at her and she pushed her paranoia and insecurity away. 'Lucas,' she said, taking his hand, 'Enrico is strong. Here—' she touched a finger to her temple '—and here.' She placed a hand over her heart. 'He has much he yet wants to see come to fruition and more he wishes to achieve.'

Dark eyes throbbed into hers.

'He has a lot to live for and he's getting the very best medical care. Take heart from that and don't give up hope.'

With a nod, he squeezed her hand before releasing it.

She hugged him before he went through customs, and for a brief moment he held her against him as if he'd never let her go, but then he released her and stepped away. He didn't kiss her. 'I'll be in touch.'

He turned and walked away and everything inside her throbbed. But then he swung around and strode back.

Kiss me. Please.

'I forgot to give you this.'

He pressed a velvet box into her hands. *That* velvet box.

'I asked you to marry me while we were here in Australia and you accepted. Roger?'

It wasn't really a question. 'I... Okay.'

It all seemed so businesslike and cold. This

time when he turned away, he didn't look back and an icy shiver shook her, along with a horrible premonition. Would she ever see him again? If Enrico should worsen—

She couldn't bear to finish that thought. Please, God, don't let that happen. Please let Enrico live for much *much* longer yet. Not only did she wish it because the thought of never seeing Lucas again was so unbearable—even though it was— but because she loved the older man and he deserved to live a long and happy life.

She tried not to fret over the next couple of days. Lucas sent her a couple of hasty texts keeping her abreast of Enrico's condition. The older man was weak but improving slowly every day, and she gave thanks for it.

Lucas's absence, though, was a physical ache. She had to sit when she realised why. And then laughed at herself for it having taken so long to sink in. She'd fallen in love with him. Again. Or maybe she'd never fallen out of love with him. Having found their way back to one another felt like a miracle. She couldn't lose him again. She just couldn't.

Lucas found himself returning to Hallie's studio in the palazzo again and again over the next few days as they waited—and prayed—for Enrico to recover his strength. The studio was the place he felt closest to her. He missed her like...

Like the piece that had been missing from him for the past seven years.

In Sydney things had changed between them and it wasn't just the fact that they'd given in to temptation and made love. His mouth dried at the memory of their lovemaking. It had been intense and passionate, warm and playful, tender. It had been *everything*.

Long-standing misunderstandings had been resolved and old hurts had started to heal. Even now the weight that had been lifted from him shocked him to his marrow. He hadn't realised he'd been struggling under such a load.

At the appointed time, he set up his laptop and dialled Hallie's number. When her face appeared on his screen, he let out a breath he hadn't known he'd been holding. 'I've missed you,' he said before even greeting her.

Anxious eyes roved over his face and then she smiled. Which made his heart beat at the right tempo again. 'I've missed you, too. *So* much. And I'm glad Enrico is doing so well. You must all be enormously relieved.'

'I feel as if I can breathe again—as if my brain once again works.' His grandfather's hospital stay may even prove a blessing in disguise as the specialists had placed him on a clinical trial for a new drug. It wouldn't cure him, but the doctors were optimistic that it would extend his life.

A month ago, that would've presented him and

Hallie with a new challenge—how to negotiate their fake engagement for a longer period of time than originally expected. But now…

Something a lot like happiness and hope rose through him. Now nothing about their relationship felt fake. 'He told me to send you his love.'

'And give him mine.'

Picking up his laptop, he carried it to an Alice chair—*her* Alice chair. He fancied if he breathed deeply enough he could catch a trace of her scent. She peered beyond him and smiled. 'Are you in the studio?'

He shrugged. 'I like it up here. It makes me feel closer to you. Did I mention I miss you?'

She gurgled out a laugh. 'Same, and believe me, I'll be counting down the next three days.'

When she returned to Venice. He couldn't wait. 'I wish I'd booked you on a flight earlier in the week.' He shifted and something rustled behind his back.

'I'll be there before you know it,' she promised.

He had visions of himself counting down every single hour. Pulling a notepad out from behind the cushion, he went to set it on the table when his gaze caught on the heading at the top of the page. He froze.

Reasons why I shouldn't be with Lucas.

'Now tell me how everyone else is doing? Is Juliet getting excited about her upcoming concert?'

Reasons why I shouldn't be with Lucas.

Something inside his chest fractured as he read down the list of reasons why Hallie didn't think he was the man for her.

'Lucas, is everything okay?' Concern threaded through her voice. 'Have you just received bad news or… Are you feeling ill?'

He felt sick to his stomach. And a fool. Such a fool.

He held the list up so she could see it. 'When were you going to tell me about this?'

Even from half a world away, he could see the blood drain from her face. 'Lucas, I can explain. I—'

He cut the connection. He didn't want to hear. He didn't want to be taken in by her lies or listen to her excuses. For her, agreeing to their arrangement had been a way of drawing a line under the past so she could move on. He glanced at the list he still held. How had she phrased it? *Closure and a new start.* A new start that clearly didn't include him.

Dropping the list to the table, he rose and left the room, closing the door behind him.

* * *

Lucas spent the next day in a kind of limbo—
a black pit of nothingness, an abyss. He locked
himself away in his office in the palazzo and sat
at his desk. Time moved in odd sluggish surges.
An hour or a minute, they felt the same.

He couldn't recall feeling like this seven years
ago.

He remembered the stinging shock of the
words Hallie had flung at him as she'd left him
seven years ago. *'I've lost faith in this.'* Her *this*
had referred to them, to him? He remembered
crushing pain and denial. But he didn't remember numbness or this listless apathy, the utter
lack of energy.

By the next morning, pain had started to filter
in around his edges and he imagined he could
actually feel the fracture lines cracking all the
way through him until he was nothing but a vio-
lent, throbbing ache. He wondered what colour
Hallie would paint it and started to laugh.

His laughter held no humour. It sounded
harsh and ugly in the soft morning light and he
snapped his mouth shut to cut it off.

But thinking about ugliness and colour and
pain and how Hallie would depict them on canvas made him remember what he'd buried deep
in his closet. Flinging the bedclothes back, he
strode across to the huge walk-in affair and
stared at the package resting on a top shelf.

He reached up and then stopped. He needed a shower and a change of clothes and maybe even a shave before he faced that. He might feel like hell, but he didn't have to look like it.

Half an hour later, he marched into Hallie's studio, package in hand. Cutting the twine and pulling away the layers of wrapping, he set the portrait sketch Hallie had done of him in February to an Alice chair. Hands on hips, he surveyed it.

Technically, it was extraordinary. But he didn't care about technique. He stared at the man in that portrait and his jaw clenched. Why the hell would Hallie fall for that man? He was *awful*.

He paced around the studio three times like a caged tiger, before halting in front of the sketch again. Why would Hallie fall in love with someone like that? No one would.

His hands clenched and unclenched. Except that wasn't the face he'd presented to her in recent weeks, and it sure as hell wasn't the face he'd presented to her in Sydney a week ago!

Still… He glared at the canvas. Why would she risk it? What if he turned back into that beast?

He wouldn't. He'd learned his lesson. But why on earth would she believe that?

Seizing the list she'd made, he read down each item.

1. Lucas considered my miscarriage a blessing in disguise.

No, he hadn't! And she knew that now—knew he'd mourned the loss of the child they hadn't had.

2. He will never forgive me for breaking his heart.

Again, not true. She had to know that, right?

3. We want different things.

He scrubbed a hand through his hair. Did they? He'd thought they were finally on the same page again. There'd been no chance to talk about what their future might hold, though, before he'd had to race back to Venice. Maybe they weren't on the same page at all.

4. He has a seriously bad temper.

He swore. He had to take that one on the chin. His temper might only be bad around her, but it didn't change the fact that she'd borne the brunt of it more than once. He'd apologised. But maybe she'd chosen to hold it against him.

5. Apparently I'm evil—the devil incarnate— a seductress!

He groaned.
There was an accompanying cartoon drawing.

She made an adorable devil, draped in jewels and batting oversize eyelashes. He suspected he was the ridiculous stomping, scowling, steam-coming-out-of-his-ears figure nearby. Why had he acted like such an idiot?

6. He can't see or acknowledge that he broke my heart, too.

Wrong. He thrust out his jaw. *So* wrong.

7. He runs hot and cold. When he kissed me, he treated it like a misdemeanour of monumental proportions.

He dragged a hand across his nape, scowling. He'd been so ashamed of leaping on her like he had. Ashamed of not keeping his baser instincts under control. Ashamed of taking advantage of her when all she'd tried to do was support him.

There were other items on her list, too. But… he could work on his faults, couldn't he? He could become the man she wanted—a better man. If only she'd give him a chance.

And if she won't?

He braced his hands on his knees as his chest cramped. How would they negotiate their fake engagement? How would he cope seeing her every day and…

Very slowly, he straightened, shook his head.

He wouldn't. Reaching for his phone he rang his lawyer and directed him to have the deeds of the building he'd promised Hallie to be transferred into her name. She'd done all that he'd asked of her, and he wouldn't let her lose out financially, but he refused to continue with this charade.

If she didn't love him the way he loved her—or if there was no chance of winning her love—then he couldn't put himself through it. And he wouldn't put her through it, either.

Could he win her love and convince her to give them a second chance? Growing up, she'd never been the centre of anyone's universe—not in the way he'd been the centre of his mother's life, or in the way the Zaneris made him feel like the beating heart of the family. Her father lived for his work, while her mother had lived for him. And when she'd realised the futility of that, she hadn't been able to go on. Not even for her teenage daughter.

Seven years ago had he selfishly expected to be at the centre of Hallie's world without making her the centre of his? She'd always felt like his centre, he'd needed her, but had he made sure she'd known that? Had he made her feel cherished?

Very slowly, he shook his head. He hadn't. He'd been a fool.

But could he make her feel cherished now?

Could he convince her to take a chance on him again?

He stared at the sketch. He wasn't that man any more. And—

'You absolutely infuriating pig-headed man!'

He swung around to find Hallie *bristling* in the doorway. He pinched himself. 'You're not due to arrive until tomorrow.' Or had he lost a day somewhere?

She dropped her hand luggage to the floor and glared. 'As you refused to listen to my explanation on our video call, I changed to an earlier flight.'

'But—'

'Oh, don't you *but* me.' Her eyes flashed. 'You, who claims to value faith so highly. Yet, you'd believe that I'd make love with you—open myself up and be vulnerable to you—while keeping that kind of list?'

The expression on her face... He started breathing again. Cracks inside him started closing up. He couldn't speak for the relief.

Moving across, she snatched the list he still held and shook it in his face. 'I started keeping this list back in February.'

'You've added to it while you've been here,' he couldn't help pointing out.

'In an attempt to keep some emotional distance from you. So I'd remember our deal was a business arrangement, despite the pretence we were putting on.' She scrunched the list up into a little ball. 'Because I couldn't afford to let myself forget that you didn't like me. That you, in fact, loathed me.'

'I don't any more!'

'I know! Which is why I stopped keeping this stupid thing!' She threw the list across the room.

His heart hammered against his ribs.

'But now you're going to go back to being all cold and remote and wounded.'

'No, I'm not.'

She stilled and glanced up.

He gestured between them. 'You and I are going back to square one. So two things…'

'We're what?'

'And the first of those things is that I rang my lawyer and directed him to put the deeds of the building in your name. You don't need to worry that you'll be inheriting the costs for the building repairs, either. They've been taken care of.'

Her eyes narrowed. 'Why would you do that?'

'And the second thing…' He gestured to the third finger of her left hand and the ring she wore, and held out his hand.

Her eyes sheened with tears, but she hitched up her chin, tugged the ring from her finger and slapped it into his palm.

Through the pain crushing her chest, Hallie was distantly aware of Lucas's frown.

'But… You never liked this ring.'

She hadn't. 'Way too flashy.' She turned and marched across to the French windows, but barely registered the view of the canal below. How could he expect her to be happy, though, when he was calling everything off?

She supposed she ought to be glad. Feeling the way she did about him, she doubted she'd be able to maintain their engagement pretence. She'd probably keep bursting into floods of tears, which was a pathetic thought.

'And now we're back at square one.'

Meaning what? Turning, she found him sauntering towards her, a strange intent in his eyes.

'There are now no business deals existing between us and no fake engagements—nothing to muddy the waters.'

Her heart gave a silly little flip. 'What waters?'

'Don't you feel as if we were always meant to be, Hallie? You and me?'

She had. And then she hadn't. And now…

'I've loved you from the first moment I saw you walk into that pub.'

He… *What?*

'I tried to dress it up in uglier emotions when you left, but…' He trailed off. 'These last few weeks have been a revelation, a challenge, and exhilarating beyond measure.'

What was he saying?

He went down on one knee and her heart clenched and her pulse did a crazy dance. 'Hallie, will you please marry me? If you say yes, I'll spend the rest of my life making sure you know that you're the centre of my universe.'

The room blurred. The only thing that remained in focus was Lucas's face—strong and steady. In his fingers he held a ring—*her* ring. The ring she'd treasured from the moment he'd slid it onto her finger all those years ago. The ring she'd thought she'd wear for ever. The ring it had broken her heart to return.

'I love you, Hallie, heart and soul. I promise to spend every day proving to you just how much, and doing all I can to make you happy.'

Warmth radiated through her chest. Her entire being went weightless. Seizing his arms, she pulled him to his feet. 'No, Lucas, *we* will spend the rest of our lives making *each other* happy.'

He blinked as if trying to make sense of her words.

'You see, I made another list…a list of all of the reasons I wanted you in my life.' She pulled it from her back pocket, practically dancing on the spot. 'Reasons to be with Lucas,' she recited. 'One. He's wonderful with his family and has a great relationship with them all.'

She turned it to show him the accompanying illustration of him and Juliet. He had her in a headlock, ruffling her hair while she tried to squirm free. It was full of affection and fun, and his lips hooked up. She wondered if her feet were even touching the ground.

'Two. He defended me when some members of his family were wary and less than welcoming, proving that he's a man of his word and keeps his promises.'

She glanced up to find his eyes throbbing with barely contained emotion. She rustled her page to make sure it was her words that still held his attention. 'Three. The man *does* dance better than me.'

A laugh choked out of him.

'Four. He has time for fun things like water polo. I never thought I'd see that day—my bad.'

Something in his eyes softened.

'Five. He's fun and has a great sense of humour.'

She showed him the drawings of their fake dates when they'd gone sightseeing and the night of the opera. He reached out to trace a finger across them.

'Six. He's a good friend. He supported me through the devastation of the fire at my studio. Seven. He's a generous lover.' She pulled in a breath. 'And eight. Nobody makes me feel like he does when we're together. He's the palette to my paintbrush, the sun to my moon, the piece of me I never knew was missing.'

He stared at her as if he didn't know what to

say. That was okay. She had words enough for both of them. She smiled then. It burst from her like sunshine. 'That's a yes, by the way, Lucas.' Reaching up on tiptoe, she pressed her lips to his. 'I can't think of anything I want more than to marry you, to build a life with you and have a family with you.'

Wonder crossed his face then and fresh tears brimmed in her eyes. With a whoop, he lifted her off her feet and swung her around. Throwing her head back, she laughed for the sheer joy of it.

'You have made me the happiest of men!' He set her back on her feet and slid the ring onto her finger. It sparkled as if it was exactly where it belonged. The happiness radiating from him warmed her to her very bones.

'I'm sorry I was such an idiot, Hallie. That I didn't let you explain about the list the other day. I was shocked at how hurt I felt, how devastated… and that's when I realised I'd fallen in love with you again. I've been up here this morning trying to come up with ways to convince you to take another chance on me, on us.'

'No convincing necessary.' Reaching up, she cupped his face in her hands. 'I love you, Lucas. With all of me. For ever.'

His face gentled. 'Hallie…'

'You want to make me happy?'

Reaching up, he took her hands in his and held them as if they were precious. 'I do.'

'Then no more blame, no more regrets. We have a chance for a fresh start, to go into the future with hope and optimism and love.' *So much love.* 'Let's cherish that and make the most of it.'

'No more blame, no more regrets,' he promised. 'I mean to treasure all that we have. It's doubly precious to me now.'

Oh, Lord, he'd have her in floods soon. 'I think you'd better kiss me,' she whispered.

'Excellent idea.'

As his head bent towards hers, she reached out and pinched his forearm.

He blinked. 'What was that for?'

'This is a *major* pinch-me moment. I want us to remember it for ever.'

His grin, when it came, curled her toes. 'I'm planning on giving you a lifetime full of pinch-me moments, Hallie.'

She grinned then, too. Reaching up on tiptoe, she whispered, 'I'm going to hold you to that.'

And then she kissed him. And as the kiss was the best of her life, she pinched herself, too.

EPILOGUE

Fifteen months later

As THEY FINISHED singing 'Happy Birthday', and Enrico blew out the candles on his ridiculously large and over-the-top birthday cake—a wicked concoction consisting of layers of chocolate sponge, fresh cream and cherries—a funny pain gripped Hallie's chest. To be able to call this family her own—to be part of so much warmth and love—was a dream come true. And it was every bit as wonderful as she'd always dreamed.

She and Lucas had married fourteen months ago—neither of them had seen any reason to wait. It had been a quiet family affair and all the more precious for the fact that it had meant so much to everyone in their close-knit circle.

And, of course, it had given so much happiness to Enrico. They'd confessed their earlier fake relationship arrangement to him and he'd chortled in delight, wagging a finger at them.

'Fate, *cari cuori*...' Dear hearts. 'You are soul-mates. You were always meant to be.'

She ran a hand across her oversize belly. To be able to add to this family as well now... She had to blink hard as the edges of the room blurred. It was all too wonderful for words!

Lucas, constantly vigilant, constantly attentive, set a generous slice of cake that she had no hope of getting through in front of her. He rested his hand over hers on her belly. Whenever he did that, a sense of wonder stole over his face. It sent another funny twinge of happiness rippling through her—starting at her centre and rippling outwards. The look on his face the first time he'd felt one tiny leg kick... Even now it had the power to make her feel a little weak at the knees.

When she'd told him she was pregnant, he'd cried. They both had. He would make the most wonderful father—in the same vein as Enrico—loving and kind, a man who'd set a good example, a man who'd demand the best from and for his children.

Her gaze strayed to Massimo sitting quietly at the far end of the table. *Quiet* was a word that described him perfectly. He visited Enrico every week and attended all the family events and dinners that he was invited to, but he kept himself very much in the background.

He'd upgraded his living arrangements and

now rented a tiny flat. He'd trained as a counsellor and continued to work for the charity that had helped him in so many ways. Enrico had set up a trust to support the charity and to everyone's surprise, Lucas had agreed to be a trustee.

'I no longer wish to be ruled by bitterness or resentment,' he'd told her later. 'I've looked into the charity and it does good work. I'm happy to give my support to such a worthwhile cause.'

She'd hugged him—rather fiercely—and he'd kissed her, and it had been a long time before either of them came up for air.

She'd come to appreciate Massimo's wry humour, his clear-eyed realism and his self-deprecation. And as he always brought her and Rosa a delicious box of handcrafted chocolates whenever he visited, she was disposed to like him. She and Lucas had also spoken about what role Massimo might play in their children's lives.

'Our children will have you and me to give them stability, Lucas—to provide them with all the love and care they need. And they have Fran and Rosa for that, too, if needed.'

His lips had kinked into a smile. 'Why do I feel there's a *but* coming?'

'Grandparents are different to parents and I want our children to have everything that's in our power to give them. Including grandparents—and as there's only one around...'

'Massimo,' he'd sighed.

'I have no issue if he wishes to dote on and spoil our children. Do you?'

She'd watched him carefully, holding her breath. He eventually nodded. 'You're right. It's a thing apart from me.'

She hadn't known it was possible to love him even more until that moment.

'Is everything okay?' he asked her now, glancing at her untouched cake. 'Is there anything I can get you?'

'Everything is wonderful.'

Reaching across, she pinched him lightly and he laughed. His gaze turned to Enrico and he nodded. 'It's a miracle.'

Enrico had exceeded even the doctors' most hopeful expectations—the drug trial had proved a success. Every day that he remained with them was a gift.

Lucas turned back to her. 'Have you made a decision about the Scandinavian royal family yet?'

They'd requested she paint a portrait for them—not their official portrait, but a less formal and more family-oriented one—one for *them* rather than the state. It would be her most prestigious commission to date and had her ridiculously excited. If they could agree on terms. 'I've told them I'll do it if they wait six months.' She ran a hand over her belly again. 'I know it's not necessary but I want to take six months maternity leave.' And she wasn't giving that up for anyone. No matter how amazing the commission.

'Hold firm. They'll agree to your terms. Your portraits are amazing and worth waiting for. They know that.'

Another wave of happiness squeezed her silly. This man was so good for her ego. He had so much faith in her.

She frowned and shifted. Darn it. Happiness wasn't supposed to hurt this much, and—

Oh.

'Lucas,' she whispered.

But he was listening to something an exuberant Juliet was describing in dramatic detail.

'Lucas,' she whispered a little louder.

He bent an ear towards her, his eyes still on Juliet and his lips curving at her antics. 'Mm?'

Maybe they could slip away quietly without causing a scene. 'I'm having contractions,' she whispered.

'You're in labour?' he hollered, shooting to his feet so fast he knocked his chair over.

The place erupted and she started to laugh. So much for slipping away. 'Calm down, everyone. It's fine. It'll be hours away yet and—'

She groaned as another pain gripped her, hard and fierce and strong. Oh, Lordy Lord. 'Get me to the hospital, Lucas. *Now.*'

* * *

Fourteen hours later Lucas gazed at her with a mixture of awe and love. 'You're amazing—the most amazing woman that ever lived.'

She chuckled at his nonsense. He was as euphoric as she was on whatever happy hormones currently flooded her system.

'No, Hallie.' He shook his head, oddly serious. 'You've made all of my dreams come true. You've given me things I never knew I wanted, given me things I never knew I was missing. I'll never be able to thank you for that.' His hand gripped hers. 'I love you.'

He gazed at her with such loving intensity, her eyes filled with tears.

'Happy?' he whispered.

'So happy,' she breathed. 'So *very* happy.'

She gazed down at the tiny bundle sleeping peacefully in her arms. They'd named him Enrico in honour of his great-grandfather. A fact that would delight the older man when they told him. Little Rico had a headful of strawberry blonde curls and was perfect in every single way. Love billowed in her chest.

'How is little Jasmine doing over there?' she whispered. Rico's sister had been born twenty-five minutes after him, and was named after Hallie's mother. She had a shock of dark hair and dark, inquisitive eyes just like her daddy.

'She is divine.'

Hallie couldn't agree more.

'She will grow up as smart and intelligent as her mother. They both will.'

'And they'll also grow up as beautiful and generous as their father.'

Grinning stupidly at each other, they reached out and pinched each other's arms.

* * * * *

*If you enjoyed this story,
check out these other great reads
from Michelle Douglas*

Secret Fling with the Billionaire
Tempted by Her Greek Island Bodyguard
Claiming His Billion-Dollar Bride
Waking Up Married to the Billionaire

All available now!